THE RULING CLASS

★

Other books by Francine Pascal

My Mother Was Never a Kid
My First Love and Other Disasters
Love & Betrayal & Hold the Mayo
The Hand-Me-Down Kid

Series
Fearless FBI
Fearless
Sweet Valley High
Caitlin

★

For **Anita Elliott Anastasi,**
whose name I shamelessly stole,
and **Molly Wenk** for her invaluable help.

★

Thanks to Tom and Sara McQuaid and family for all the Dallas information. And for assorted help, thank you to Mia and Nicole Johansson, Alice Wenk, John Carmen, Hilary Bloom, Genevieve Gagne-Hawes, Jon Marans, David Bryan, and my dream editor, Paula Wiseman. And, as always, for wise advice and support, my agent of twenty-five years, Amy Berkower.

THE RULING CLASS

★

Beauty fades, but dumb is forever.

—Judge Judy

Myrna Fry Speaking

CHAPTER 1

My dream has so come true. Totally. I've only been waiting since my first day in high school, and I'm a junior now, but I don't care how long it took, it was way worth it. It's all about Jeanette Sue, even the name is gorgeous, you have to see her—she's, like, fantastic. Every bag she has is either Kate Spade or Coach or Vuitton, and she wouldn't put her big toe, which has the most fabulous gold and diamond ring on it, into anything that wasn't at least Jimmy Choos or Manolos or better. She has four Harry Winston chains with silver links and one Tiffany bracelet with a tiny charm with her name on it. I mean, she's all Diesel or Gaultier or Armani, and everything looks, like, fabulous because she's got a to-die-for figure. And she only smokes these long, skinny, wicked Vogue cigarettes and she sort of, like, flips her hair, a quick back-forth, when she exhales, so that the smoke kind of goes all over like a cloud around her face, which looks fabulous when she wears her Von Dutch hat.

You know all that baloney about smoking being addictive and causing cancer and all? Not true. Rush Limbaugh said so on the radio. It absolutely hasn't really been proved yet.

On top of all that she's part of the horsey set, a champion jumper. Like, she won the blue ribbon two years in a row at the Fairmont Riding Club. That's the most totally elegant horse club in Dallas. In fact, she has her own horse.

Anyway, with her so blond hair (somebody said it's not really blond, but they don't know) and her aqua eyes (I heard they're color contacts, but I don't believe that) and the whitest teeth (this girl in my math class said they're all caps, but that's not true), she's way the most perfect girl in the school.

And everybody knows she's so the absolute queen. Now get this, the queen has invited me to have lunch with her and her whole gang today. These are not just regular nobody people, these are the absolute coolest guys at Highland Park High. She just asked me yesterday and I've been going so nuts ever since.

She sort of suggested that it was going to be like a picnic and I should bring some sandwiches. She said probably there would be about six of us. I hope everyone likes ham. If they don't, like if somebody doesn't eat meat, I made some tuna salad. Well, not exactly me, the maid, but I told her to do it.

And then if somebody else, like maybe a couple of the other cheerleaders, drops by, I threw in some extra stuff, like some peaches, but no bananas. Everyone knows that South American bananas are contaminated with that flesh-eating disease. Whatever. What with all the sodas, no Dr Pepper; I know for a fact that they put out a special-edition can that had the Pledge of Allegiance and they took out the "under God" part. Anyway, I had to buy an assortment, and I've been lugging this huge Armani shopping bag around all morning. But I so don't mind. I'm, like, totally excited that she chose me. I mean, this is blast-me-out major.

We're supposed to meet under the big pear trees on the back lawn behind the school. Somebody planted them when they first built the school, and now they're fully grown, and the way they've got them, like, in two lines facing each other, they sort of form a tunnel. Even though they never have pears, which seems, like, really dumb for a pear tree, still they make a perfect tent for a picnic. And you really need shade down here in Dallas when it gets closer to summer, that sun is totally like a ball of fire. It's such a bore how they're always going on about the ozone layer, how it's getting, like, holes in it 'cause of spray cans. Hello. Like I'm really going to stop using hair spray just 'cause of global warming. Gimme a break. Who doesn't love warm weather?

Anyway, all this was actually a desert before everybody came here. That's what my boring history teacher said. You should see her, my teacher I mean, she has the hairiest legs and she never shaves them. Even though her name is McGrady, I think she's really Spanish, because everybody knows how hairy they are. It's, like, from all the oil they eat. Or she could be Romanian, I never actually saw a Romanian, but I heard they're hairy too. Everybody knows most for-eigners are hairy. That's what my family always says and we're real Americans, so we know. Anyway, somebody must have added a lot of dirt to the ground, because now we have these rolling green lawns that make our high school look like something out of a movie. Like I should care.

Even though it's a public school, it's in a very rich neighborhood and they do a lot of private financing, so we have everything just like the best private schools. I mean, we have this fabulous pool and tennis courts and of course a football stadium for the Highlanders, our championship team, and a theater and everything. And because it's Dallas and the weather is mostly not really cold in the winter, we have flowers with stupid names like bougainvillea and impatiens all year. It looks like the best country club you could find, and it acts like that too. You have to live in the neighborhood to get in.

That's the catch. If you're going to live in the neighborhood, you have to buy a house for at least a million dollars, and most of them cost even more, so that means only the right people would be living here anyway. My house is one of the ones that just makes it, only a million two. I mean, we're on the right street, Preston Road, but ours is the cheapest house on the block. My stepfather is a lawyer for the oil companies, and he's always bragging that that's the best thing to be, the cheapest house in the neighborhood. I think he's an asshole and I hate our house. I wish my mother were prettier so she could have married someone richer.

Anyway, because Highland Park is a public school, they have to do that integration stuff, like they have to take some poor kids from the Vickery houses, that's about a mile away, around Eastridge Street. They have really crappy houses there, and you can pick out the kids easy. They are so not HighlandPark, they don't stand a chance. They just come to school and then they disappear and nobody knows where they go and nobody cares. At least we don't, the real people who belong here.

Jeanette Sue said twelve o'clock, but classes got out at eleven forty-five so I didn't even stop to pee. I just came right out here. I guess I'm way early, but that's okay.

I'm not sure, but I think I probably won't try to sit next to Jeanette Sue today. That would be a little much for the first time. Maybe I should sit next to Joanne Wilson, she's only just got in the group, and I don't know how because she's got these ugly freckles all over her arms. Ugh! I suppose it goes with the red hair. I personally have nothing against the Irish, it's just that I don't want the pope moving in next door to me. You know how they have those four million children. But I'm not saying she is, just that if I did sit next to her, I wouldn't look so pushy. Or maybe Anna Marie, but no, she's like Jeanette Sue's clone, and besides she never liked me. I don't want to take any chances on my first day.

I didn't even think Jeanette Sue knew I was alive. I mean, she's never even talked to me except once when she forgot her geometry book, so I loaned her mine. Dumb-ass teacher gave me an extra homework assignment for being unprepared, but it was so worth it.

Actually, she never gave it back—Jeanette Sue, I mean. But that was okay, all I had to do was go down to the supply room and tell them some dumb story and pay twenty dollars, and they gave me another one.

The next day I said hello to Jeanette Sue, but I guess she didn't hear me.

Anyway, today is totally fabulous. Imagine Myrna Fry, that's me, absolutely nobody, having lunch with the Ruling Class. That's what everyone calls them. It's so the best clique in the whole school. I mean, they've got the cheerleaders, the basketball and football stars, plus all the greatest people, including last year's homecoming queen, which of course just happens to be Jeanette Sue.

I can't believe how way lucky I am. Like I said, it's been my dream, me and Jeanette Sue, just hanging together. Going horseback riding together and sleeping over and all that and, like, eating pizza and watching *The Ring* for the hundredth time or *American Pie*. And then staying up till four in the morning and talking about boys. All this at her house, of course. Mine would be okay except it's got my parents in it.

Being part of the RCs, that's what everyone calls them, is everything I ever wanted.

I can't believe the time. It's almost ten to one, I guess they all got held up. It's going to have to be a quick picnic, lunch hour is over in ten minutes. They're not going to have much time to eat all those sandwiches. . . .

Oh, I see them! Over there near the back entrance. They're all there: Joanne Wilson, I can see her red hair, and Anna Marie, of course dressed exactly like Jeanette Sue. Sometimes she wears jodhpurs even though she doesn't even ride, and Kathy Diggers, because she's so tall you can spot her anywhere, and Maryanne Tobby and Betty Jane Oborne. Except for Joanne they all have blond hair or blond streaks, like copies of Jeanette Sue. And I can see them looking in my direction. And pointing. I wave so that they'll know it's me.

Something must be funny, because they're all standing there and even from here I can see they're laughing.

Oh God, they don't know it's me. They're leaving. How gross is that?

"Hey!" I go. "I'm here! Over here!" I'm waving like crazy, but they mustn't see me, because they're walking away.

Damn! They're going back into the school!

I grab the shopping bag and start running, shouting, "Wait up!" but dragging that heavy bag slows me up, and by the time I get there, they've gone inside.

And the door is locked. They never lock this back door, but this time they must have, because I can't budge it. It's like it's stuck from the inside. I'm pulling like crazy but it won't open. It's like I can hear people inside, at least it sounds like somebody's there, but they don't seem to hear me.

Even if I go around the front, they'll be gone by the time I get to the back. I missed them. And now they're probably going to think I purposely didn't show up, like I think I'm too good for them, and maybe they'll never invite me again. I so missed my whole chance. I just know it.

I just hate my mother. Yeah, I know she didn't exactly have anything to do with this, but I can just hear her going on about how I probably screwed it up because I so didn't listen. That's her big thing, how I'm not a good listener. Ever since I was a little kid, it's like it's the most important thing in the world. She was always comparing me with some other kid who of course was always a good listener. Naturally she never stops talking long enough to listen to me.

In history class I try to explain to Jeanette Sue what happened, how I must have misunderstood where we were going to meet, but that I was really there and didn't stand anyone up, and please not to think I would do that, especially not to her.

And she goes, "Well, we waited for you."

"Under the pear trees?"

"No, dummy, I told you in the lunchroom."

By now Anna Marie, Maryanne, Betty Jane, Joanne, and Kathy Diggers—she's the most stuck-up girl in the RCs, just because one time she rode on a float in the Orange Bowl Parade. She's always talking about it, like everything is, "When I was in the parade, we did this and we did that." Big deal, anybody could if their father was a lawyer for the Dallas Cowboys before he went to Halliburton (that's a charity group that's helping out in Iraq). Besides, she was only four at the time, how does she even remember? Anyway, they're all standing there swearing that I was supposed to meet them in the lunchroom.

And then I go, "Right, you did say the lunchroom, but I forgot. I'm really—"

"How about you listen better next time? You're getting on my last nerve, darlin', I mean it."

See that? She called me "darlin'." Even though she sort of cuts me off and sounds annoyed, still I know that's not the way she meant it. Hey, I wouldn't like being stood up by somebody.

I sort of follow them out of the classroom into the hallway, and we're all talking about this movie with Rachael Leigh Cook and Josh Hartnett. Actually, they're the ones talking, because I never saw it; I never even heard of it which is strange because I always know all the new movies, especially with big stars like that, but I don't want to be left out, so I say I liked it too.

Then Jeanette Sue goes, "What about that part where the guy washes his dog and puts it in the microwave to dry and the dog explodes?"

"Yeah, cool," Joanne Wilson says. I don't know how she ever got into the RCs with those freckles, and even though she's an only child, like I said, I think she's Irish and you know what that means—Catholic. Like they're going to try to make all the rest of us Catholic.

Everybody is agreeing, so I go, "Yeah, that was great." I don't remember it in any movie, but I know it's a true story because this girl who lives on my block, her cousin knows the guy who did it. She told me.

As soon as I say "Yeah," everyone stops talking and they turn to me and Anna Marie—who thinks she's Jeanette Sue but isn't nearly as pretty—and I happen to know that she had her streaks done in Candy's, which is a really cheap hair place, and they came out looking like somebody painted them because her hair is really dark and she put in these orangey streaks. I personally think her hair is suspiciously dark for a white person. I don't know how she got into the RCs, but anyway, she goes, "So you liked when he put his dog in the microwave?"

"Not really, but I thought, well, that's what he was going to do."

"What else did you think?" Betty Jane wants to know, like checking with Jeanette Sue. She's always looking at J. S., like for approval.

"Yeah, tell us," both Anna Marie and Maryanne say at the same time. They all seem really interested in what I have to say, except I don't know what to say. I'm scared that they're going to find out that I never saw the movie, but then Jeanette Sue, who is really way nicer than the rest of them, goes, "Leave her alone. She said she liked it. That's enough for me."

And they all agree, but then she starts in and wants to know what part I liked best. I can feel the tears coming up in my eyes and I know I have to say something. So I take a chance, "That part where he makes her laugh?"

And they all start laughing and say they loved that part too. I mean, they all get really hysterical. So I start laughing too. I feel like I'm already part of the RCs. Just then the bell rings for last period, and I take a big chance and I say to them, "See ya later."

"You wish," Jeanette Sue says, but she's still smiling, and turns and they all go off in the other direction.

"You wish" is okay. It's a kind of fun answer to "See ya later." Unless she said "Jewish." Oh God, I hope she doesn't think I'm Jewish. They're hairy too, you know.

CHAPTER 2

Myrna Fry

I dump the whole bag with all the sandwiches in the basement garbage in front of the janitor's office. I feel so bad about all of them missing their lunch because of me. I'll have to find some way to make it up to them.

By the time I get back to my social studies class, the bell has already rung and Ms. Wellman is sort of annoyed, but mostly she's busy with the new girl. I have to control myself from breaking up when I see her, the new girl. I mean, the clothes, forget it. Trailer trash. Knockoff Express. I mean, like anyone would bother to knock off Express clothes that are already crappy enough. Too much.

I giggle. I can't help it, and then Maryanne Tobby, an RC like me, practically gets hysterical. She covers her face with her Kate Spade and all you see is her long blond hair bouncing up and down. And that starts everyone else, and finally Ms. Wellman catches on and gets furious with us. She's a butthead anyway.

"Class," Ms. Wellman says, "if you can control yourselves for a minute and show some manners, I'd like to introduce you to your new classmate. This is Twyla Gay Stark."

In between the snorts and swallowed laughter everyone tries to make hello noises, and Twyla Gay sort of nods them back.

"Twyla Gay is from Lubbock." Ms. Wellman is smiling like it's a great place, but everybody knows about Lubbock.

Texas is a very big state, and that bump on the map has to be someplace in the middle of the Panhandle, which is more like Noplaceville—nothing but farmers, dry and dusty, with half-dead towns. Everyone knows that thing they say about how happiness is seeing Lubbock in your rearview mirror.

Then, my luck, she assigns her the seat right next to me. Just what I need, a loser who's going to be asking me a million lame questions and expect me to be her friend.

Twyla Gay smiles at me and takes her seat. I just turn away. She'll so get the hint.

Everything's going okay, and then Butthead Wellman says, "Myrna, why don't you show Twyla Gay the ropes."

I look up at her like, *Huh? Maybe she'll ask someone else.* But she doesn't get it and I'm stuck. It's not like Twyla Gay's such a dog, in fact, her face is okay looking, but everything else about her—like her hair looks like she slept in curlers, her clothes are really cheap looking, her shoes are way wrong, clunky like we were wearing two years ago, and then when she starts to talk, you can barely understand her. She's got, like, this moron accent from the sticks. The RCs see me with this hick and I'm the loser.

When the bell rings, I try to grab my things and hurry

out, but I can't lose her. There she is, running to catch up with me. I pretend I don't know she's there, but she follows me right into my last class. Lucky me, I got a new best friend.

I still don't look at her.

But it's worse in this class because Anna Marie is in it. Last thing I want is for her to tell Jeanette Sue I hang out with freaks. I scoot around Twyla Gay like I never saw her before in my life and practically run into Anna Marie.

"Hi," I go, real casual like, with a smile because, well, even though she doesn't like me so much, we're good friends now, but she's busy searching though her papers, so she doesn't answer. Either she didn't hear me or she thought I was talking to someone else. That happens.

Then Twyla Gay takes the empty seat next to mine and gives me a big, "Hi there," but I just pretend I don't hear her and start getting very busy with my papers.

When Anna Marie looks up, she sees me and I roll my eyes and nod toward Twyla Gay like, *Do you believe her?*

But Anna Marie doesn't respond. I think she's maybe a little cross-eyed, 'cause I swear she looks like she's looking right at me.

For the whole rest of the class I keep my head turned away from Twyla Gay. But she so doesn't get it. And when the class ends, she's on my tail again.

Even when I walk out of the school, she's there. She's, like, so ruining my afternoon. I had planned to maybe hang out with the RCs for a while. Maybe even walk Jeanette Sue home. She's only about fifteen minutes out of my way. But now I'm careful not to look around for any of them. All I need is for them to see me with this creep. I start walking fast toward my house, when I realize that my new best friend is talking to me.

Not that I can really understand what she's saying, but it sounds like she saw me walking to school this morning and she has to pass my street. Not that she lives in my neighborhood; this is definitely a Vickery house person.

"Huh?" I turn around and give her a real, like, *What are you bothering me for?* look.

She starts to repeat her story, when I cut her off. "Yeah, I get it. You have to walk past my street. Big deal."

We're just passing the coffee shop when she asks me if I want a soda. Actually, I am thirsty. I should have saved one of those sodas from lunch.

"My treat," she goes.

I make sure no one is watching. "Okay," I go, but the kind of *okay* that means "just this once."

CHAPTER 3

Twyla Gay

I can tell Myrna doesn't like me. That's okay. I'm not crazy about her, either. She's nothing like my friend Betsy or any of my good friends in Lubbock. Myrna's a real suck-up and not even that smart. If she were, she would know that I know she doesn't like me. It's almost funny the way she rolls her eyes when I ask her something. Funny thing was that other girl, the one with the streaked hair next to her in class, was doing the same thing to her, but she was too dumb to know it.

Mostly I hate Myrna-type people, but I'm stuck; I need someone and right now she's got the most possibilities. It's like when you're new, you have to get a little inside and see what's happening, and then you know where you want to be.

Actually, I know where I want to be. Back home in Lubbock with all my real friends. But that's not possible. My mom lost her job when they closed the canning factory, and we had to go down to Dallas. Her sister, my aunt Willa, lives here, and at least she can help my mom. It's not easy for Aunt Willa, either, since my uncle died. He was really young, but he had leukemia from when he was a kid and it came back. So it's nice for her to have my mother here to help out with the kids and for company, too. Of course, she needs the money, too. We all do.

But there's no way I'm going to quit school and go to work. No way. I know some people in the family think I'm selfish, but they don't know. I would do everything I could for my family, but I need to go to college first so that I can be a lawyer or something like that and make real money and not have to keep moving around just 'cause some dumb factory closes.

Myrna Fry. I don't know which is worse, her or her name. Actually, it fits her perfectly, sort of dumpy, doughy, a little undercooked looking, and kind of puppyish, like how she jumps up and down for that group of girls. I can see they're the big shots. Anyway, she's practically licking them. I probably shouldn't talk about appearance. When I looked around this morning, I didn't see anyone like me. I mean dressed like me. Certainly no belts with fringe or stupid curls I sat up since five this morning making.

Ugh. How could I think this skirt was cool?

You can see from just looking around that everybody is really rich. They're all wearing Donna Karans or Lolita Lempickas and carrying Coach or Fendi bags. That is, everybody except me. You can't tell so much with the boys, they all look sloppy poor, except their sloppy poor probably comes from Banana Republic or Hilfiger. And even the casual look in the girls is Guess? or Bebe. They're probably licking their chops waiting to blackball me from something. Anything.

Why do they send people like me to a school like this? They think they're doing us such a big favor, but it's a lame idea that just makes you feel bad.

Look at Myrna, just waiting for the chance to say something mean to me. But right now I've got to let her because this is the kind of place you have to know what you're doing just so you can survive, and I need someone who's sort of on the inside. Or at least thinks she is.

"So, like, how come you moved here, anyway?" Myrna is looking for a place to stick in how I don't belong.

"We left after my father got hanged accidentally on the clothesline." *Go do something with that one, Myrna.* It's not true. I mean, it could be, for all I know, and I wouldn't really care, since I haven't seen him since I was six months old and I don't remember him at all. But I really just say it to throw her a little off balance so she's not so in charge.

It works.

"Oh . . . ," she says, and kind of fumfers around, "you don't have a dryer?"

I go right on. "That group of girls I saw you with, they your friends?"

"The RCs? Yeah."

"What's an RC?"

"The Ruling Class. It's just a joke name that everyone calls us by."

Now it's my chance to say, "Oh . . ."

"There's just a few of us," Myrna goes on. "Jeanette Sue is sort of the leader. You see Jeanette Sue? She's that really good-looking cheerleader. The girl I was with in the hall."

The blond one who dumped you and left you standing there with your mouth hanging open? But I don't say that out loud.

All I say is, "Right."

I'm beginning to get the Myrna picture.

"What kind of shampoo do you use?" she asks me.

"Regal Strawberry. They make it from strawberry fields near where I come from. You like it? I could get you some."

"Smells like rotten fruit."

This isn't good.

I dragged four bottles of this disgusting stuff with me, and now I can wrap it up in this gross skirt, tie it with the fringe belt, and dump the whole thing in the garbage. Except I can't afford to throw everything I own away. But they're probably like the skirt and the shampoo, all wrong. Beautiful. I'd have to pay to go to the falling-down high school six blocks away from me.

Maybe I can introduce a new style—cheap and ugly.

Or maybe I can transfer to another school. Some place more like me. Except you're not allowed to. This is my district, and you have to pay to go to a school outside your district.

By now we're in front of Myrna's house. It's really big, all white stucco with black shutters and a wraparound porch and what looks like lots of property around the sides. It has the most beautiful lawn, perfectly cut like carpet, with shrubs sculptured in different animal designs. They must have all kinds of gardeners taking care of it.

"Myrna, I can see that things are sort of different here in Dallas. If you were just moving in, what would you do if you looked like me?"

"Kill myself?"

I laugh, but I think she really means it.

"No," I tell her, "what I mean is, how would you start to change? Like, my clothes?"

"Right. No offense, but they look, like, so last year."

"And my hair?"

"Off the curls. And I don't know what color you're using, but you better lose it fast."

"It's my real color."

"Too bad."

Obviously everything about me is wrong. I don't know what to say. So I just look at her. She tries to look earnest, like she wants to help me, but the enjoyment is sneaking through.

"And your accent, hey, no offense but, it's, like, really country . . . kind of sloppy, drawly . . . weird. And so too high. Like everything has a question mark at the end."

There's no stopping her. Why is she doing this? It's so mean. I know it's different in Dallas, but we're people too. I really don't want to cry in front of such a . . .

"Maybe they shouldn't make you go to this school. No offense, but you're never going to really fit in. I mean, I think you're okay, but I can tell you people like Jeanette Sue . . . well, forget it."

I just listen because if I open my mouth to speak, I probably will cry, which is a little grotesque for a sixteen-year-old, but inside I feel just like I did when I was ten and someone said something mean. Am I always going to be so babyish inside? And then, of course, I do the dumbest thing that I'm going to hate myself forever for.

"Thanks," I say. Thanks. Do you believe that? No stopping me. "That's really nice of you to try to help me."

And I flee.

But I can hear her behind me starting on how I shouldn't tell anyone about my family.

No offense, but I should have punched her in the stomach.

Well, I can always quit school and then everyone would be happy. My family and all the people who are never going to be my friends. And then I can wear all my awful clothes and talk regular to all my fellow workers at whatever factory that'll hire a sixteen-year-old dropout.

Myrna Fry

CHAPTER 4

I don't know why I should care about a loser like that, but I have this thing about helping people. Except in this case it's a waste of time. Nothing is going to make that hick cool.

Still, we—I mean Jeanette Sue and our gang—could really have fun with her. She could be like a sort of mascot. I have to let them know she's just a joke, not a real friend. I so hope nobody saw us having a soda.

When I get home, there are two messages on my machine. One is from my cousin Amy about the play she's in that I said yes to a million years ago, and the other one is from Jeanette Sue inviting me to a party she's having Saturday night. Guess which one I'm going to?

I call Jeanette Sue right back and say yes. I'll think of some excuse for Amy. I'm not going to miss this party. It's at

Jeanette Sue's house and it's really a small group, just close friends, she says. And I can bring a boy if I want. I don't actually have a boyfriend right now. Or even before right now, so I say the guy I hang out with is going up to L.A. for the weekend with his parents for a wedding. Funny how fast those lies jump into your mouth when you need them.

"You want to bring your girlfriend? The country-singer-looking person I saw you with this afternoon?"

Shit!

"Are you kidding?" I go. "That creep? I barely know her. She followed me home because the teacher made me sit next to her. She's not exactly my style."

"I thought she looked sort of interesting."

"Actually, she's not so bad . . ."

"Why don't you bring her? Eight o'clock Saturday night. And it's dressy. Be gorgeous. You know, Armani, Baby Phat, Gaultier, whatever."

I start to ask who's coming, but she's already hung up. A lot of people don't say good-bye. It's a new thing. I mean, you can see what a waste of time it would be just sitting around saying good-bye to everyone all the time.

But right now I have to think of something good to get out of going to Amy's play. My mother is probably going to make a big deal of it, because next to being a good listener, family is her big thing. Does she really think I would miss Jeanette Sue's party just because Amy is in a play and the whole family is going, since this is the first time she's out of the wheelchair? Big deal. It's not like she was planning to be a dancer or something.

The only way out is to pretend I'm sick. Too bad I wasn't just on a plane, 'cause then I could have said I got bitten by those South American spiders that they found hiding out on the toilet seats. A lot of people got really sick from that spider, you know. But I can't use that, so it'll have to be just something ordinary. I'll start with some kind of symptoms early Saturday morning. They have to be just right, not bad enough so that my mother'll stay home with me.

Oh, and damn, I have to tell Twyla Gay she's coming. I can't imagine what she's going to wear. I would lend her something, but poor people like that don't always take a lot of baths.

I just remembered I don't have her telephone number, so I can't ask her. Too bad.

Just when I'm thinking that, the phone rings and of course, my luck, it's Miss Trailer Park, so I have to ask her. And naturally she's thrilled. I lie and tell her it's casual, I can't resist. "You know," I say, "jeans or any old thing you've got. Jeanette Sue is into baggy."

The faster they dump her, the better for me.

"Meet me at my house at seven thirty," I tell her.

She starts to ask me something, but I do a Jeanette Sue and click off.

Maybe I'll get a head start with a headache tonight. I have nothing to do anyway.

Twyla Gay

Maybe I was wrong about Myrna. That was nice of her to ask me to go to the party with her tomorrow night. Except I hate people who hang up without saying good-bye.

Now, of course, my mother wants me to tell her all about my new friends. So I tell her about Myrna. She's not really interested until I tell her Myrna lives on Preston Road, then all of a sudden she's crazy about her. My mother is always very impressed with people with money. They're her idols. It's like if you have money, you must be wonderful. Just listening to me tell her about Myrna and her beautiful house, my mother starts to fix her hair and straighten her dress like she was going to be invited for a visit.

I think my mother is lovely looking, really pretty, but very understated. She always wears soft colors, and there's nothing special about her clothes that you would notice. She's sort of background looking; on purpose, I think. It's like she feels like it's kind of over for her, like she doesn't count anymore. I guess you could say she's resigned to her life.

I don't know why, to me she's got the sweetest smile and friendliest light hazel eyes, and what's nice is that pretty much whenever she looks at me, she's smiling. But I can see that she looks tired, and no wonder, she works long hours and has since I was born. Most of the time she works on the weekends and only gets Tuesdays off. But she never complains. And she never really goes out. Mostly she just stays home and reads. She reads good books too, not romance junk.

But there is something that sort of bothers me sometimes about her. It's like she has this fascination with rich people. Maybe that's from a lifetime of never having any money, just reading about it. Still, it seems so shallow, but then, I guess it's no worse than the way people are so all wrapped up in celebrities; they act like it's their own lives. For my mother it's probably the only way she's ever going to get close to any of those things. Except if I get very rich, then I'll give her everything she ever dreamed of.

Now she wants to hear a whole lot more than I really know about Myrna and her family, so to make her happy I throw in some stuff they probably have, like, three cars and a pool.

And here we are, sitting in my aunt Willa's house, which is better than the one my mother and I had in Lubbock, but it's not quite as nice as Myrna's garage, except it's probably around the same size and just as square. Why do they make houses for poor people so ugly?

And of course, my aunt's furniture doesn't help. Besides being really worn, like the couch, which is actually torn in places, everything else has skinny, pipelike legs that wiggle. And when we first arrived, it was all kind of dirty, but my mother is a clean freak, and in two days, with my help, the place was spotless—still ugly, but clean ugly. When I get finished with college and I start to make money, this house is the first thing I'm going to fix.

Even though I'm a little worried about the party tomorrow night, I got to figure they're probably not a whole lot different from the girls at my old school. Except the difference is that I went to kindergarten with most of them, so you never had to explain who you were. There were no secrets, even if you wanted to keep one; everybody knew everything about you.

And there was no such thing as not fitting in. You had your spot right from the beginning and that's where you stayed. It was okay for me, I liked mine, but I guess if you didn't, it was a long time to be stuck in the wrong place.

If I start now, maybe I can figure out what I'm wearing and not have that major last-minute panic with my whole closet on the bed. Casual should be easy. Jeans and a T-shirt. Or a blouse. Long sleeves or short. Low neck, high neck, or no neck, just straps. Straight legs, or maybe they're into flared here. I wish I had noticed today. Dark blue or bleached?

Fortunately, once I make those basic decisions, there aren't that many things to choose from. The advantages of being poor.

"Do you want some help?" It's my mom.

So I try a few things on for her. Everything she loves is so Lubbock, even I know it's way wrong. So actually she is a help. Now I can eliminate 95 percent of my wardrobe.

"I like the curls the way you have them," she says, "it's so puffy and fluffy."

From now on my mother is my fashion consultant. All I have to do is the opposite of what she likes, and I can't miss.

CHAPTER 5

Twyla Gay

I get to Myrna's house fifteen minutes early and hang around on the corner, out of sight, until it's time. At exactly seven thirty I ring the doorbell. It's one of those chime things that always sound so rich. The maid opens the door. She's got my hair. At least yesterday's, fluffy and puffy, just like my mother loves.

She holds the door open for me and I step in.

"Hello," I say. "Is Myrna home?"

Before she can answer, I hear Myrna.

"Hi!"

I look up at the top of a beautiful, curved, movielike staircase and there she is. Dazzling in red satin.

Dazzling is a little much. Myrna could never dazzle, but she sure is wearing a gorgeous red satin slinky dress. And even though you can see all those extra Krispy Kremes, she still looks pretty good. For Myrna.

I don't know what to say.

"What are you wearing?" she says to me.

"You said casual."

"I did not."

"You didn't?"

"No."

"Don't you remember? Jeanette Sue is into baggy?"

"Yeah, but not for a party at her house. Even where you come from they must get dressed up for parties."

"I guess I misunderstood. I thought it was—"

"Yeah, yeah, whatever. Look, we can't be late. You'll just have to go like that."

"I don't think I can. I mean, everybody will be dressed up . . ."

"Look, I asked a special favor of Jeanette Sue to bring you, and if you don't show, you're totally finished. I mean, nobody is going talk to you ever again. It's like an insult. You have to come."

"I can't—"

"What about me? She's going to be furious at me. You can't do this to me."

I guess I can't get her in trouble with her friends. It can't be that easy for Myrna, either.

"Okay," I say, "I'll go."

At least I made her happy. She's practically giggling.

The gardener, chauffeur, whatever, drives us over to Jeanette Sue's in a gorgeous Jaguar. I've never been inside one before; the soft beige leather seats don't look like a car, more like the beautiful living-room furniture I'm dreaming of.

We drive through this really rich area called HighlandPark, where all the houses look like mansions. Jeanette Sue's is one of the biggest, big enough to be a hotel, I think, with four white columns right out of *Gone with the Wind* and a huge lawn that goes forever. And it's got, like, its own road that goes up to the house, with a circular driveway in front. Myrna says Jeanette Sue has her own horse and that she keeps it right here. They have that much property. It's really fabulous. I wish my mother could see it, but it's better she can't. She'd be very upset to see the way I look next to Myrna.

I make a couple more attempts at me not going, but Myrna makes it like it's this major thing how terrible it would be for her. So I say okay, and she rings the doorbell.

Another maid with my puffy, fluffy hair answers the door.

Myrna knows her and says, "Hello, Teresa," and scoots right past her.

Teresa turns around and looks at her really weird like. Like she's surprised to see Myrna or like it's the wrong day or something.

Myrna pays no attention to the maid and keeps going, motioning me to follow her.

The house is gigantic, with ceilings that come up to a peak like in a church. I poke my head into the one room, and some of the windows are even stained glass. I never saw a house like this outside of a movie. My mother would die just to see the inside. Well, maybe if Jeanette Sue and I got really friendly, maybe one day she could.

But I don't think we'll be that kind of good friends. There's something about Jeanette Sue that I don't think I'll like so much. Part of that something is that she's probably not going to like me that much. I'm too poor for her. That's okay; she's too rich for me.

We go down the hallway to the patio, where the music is

FRANCINE PASCAL

coming from. We can hear the people but we can't see them; still, it sounds like tons of kids. I thought this was supposed to be a small, just-close-friends party.

Myrna Fry

It sounds great. Bigger than I thought, but that's even better. I can't wait to see what happens when they see Twyla Gay in her gorgeous outfit. Gimme a break, they're going to go nuts.

Twyla Gay

I wish I were dead. This is so awful, I never should have let her talk me into going dressed like this. I am so weak and feeble sometimes, I just hate myself. It's like I'm not freak enough for this crowd, I have to go and make myself weird, too.

Myrna starts pushing open the doors. It's this double-door thing, and she pushes both doors at the same time like it's this big star entrance.

I'm trying to stay behind her, but she doesn't let me. She keeps pulling me up to her.

She shoves the doors open, and wow! It's like a million people, like the whole school, all jammed into this gigantic, fabulous outdoor room with colored lights and music and all, like it was a real disco.

It is a star entrance because as soon as the doors are wide open, like they were just waiting for us for a surprise birthday or something, everyone stops talking and turns around to look up at us on this little landing. Even the music stops.

Oh, my God!

They're all dressed like me! All except Myrna!

She's, like, frozen to the spot.

The first one to speak is Jeanette Sue, all pretend sweet

30

and friendly in her low-rise—and I mean, like, the lowest-cut back without seeing butt crack I've ever seen outside a magazine. Her top is all tight stretch multicolored spangles, which must have cost a million dollars. She's really tall and slim with, like, a mile of absolutely flat stomach between the blouse and the jeans, with sparkles in her belly button. I'm close enough to see the hickey on her shoulder.

"Myrna, I just love your dress." And then she turns around to everyone. "Don't you just love that color?"

"Cool," Joanne Wilson agrees right away.

And everyone starts calling out smart-ass things and laughing.

Myrna still hasn't moved, except now her face is the same color as her dress.

And then Jeanette Sue asks her where she got it. But it's like Myrna's mouth is glued shut. She looks like she's trying to open it but the lips are stuck. Then Jeanette Sue asks her again. This time she manages to get it open, but nothing comes out.

Actually, this is horrible, and it's not even happening to me. I'm pretty safe; I've got myself practically plastered against the wall, so nobody really sees me. Besides, I look like everyone else. I really do. It's the first time since I got to Dallas where I look like everyone else, and it's wonderful. I love it.

Except it's terrible to watch this kind of thing, even though I'm not so crazy about Myrna. In fact, when I think about it, how come she told me to wear casual? Made a big thing about baggy. Unless, of course, she was planning to do this same thing to me.

I'll bet she was. I don't know. Maybe it's too mean even for her. But maybe it's not. It sure isn't for Jeanette Sue, and she's supposed to be her friend. I think Myrna meant to make me the fun of the party. Yeah, she's a real asshole, but the joke's on her. Still, it's like watching a car wreck.

I'm thinking these things when suddenly, like a red blur, Myrna spins around and goes flying back down the hallway.

Everyone starts moaning, "Hey, get her back," "I love the dress," and stuff like that.

I'm hoping they're not going to notice me, but just to make sure, I sort of slide along the wall until I'm away from the door, and then I turn and beat it down the hallway after Myrna.

She's out the front door and halfway up the driveway. When I catch up to her, she's on her cell phone getting her driver to bring the car back.

I want to say something, but she won't even look at me.

So we both stand there pretending we're alone. Every once in a while she sniffles and gets out a tissue and blows her nose, but I know she's really wiping her eyes.

"Myrna!"

It's Jeanette Sue and her hangers-on, all sort of imitations of her, same long, straight hairstyle and expensive, sexy clothes. Betty Jane, Anna Marie, and Maryanne Tobby are from my class. Anna Marie, practically a mirror image of Jeanette Sue, is the one who got so hysterical when she first saw me—anyway, they're running toward us.

"Come on back," she says. "It was only a little joke. We wouldn't have done it if you weren't our good friend."

And the other two girls say, "Yeah, come on, we love you."

And then Jeanette Sue starts to really lay it on, and you can see dumb Myrna falling for it. Nobody has even looked at me, thank God.

Twyla Gay

Just then Myrna's car pulls up, and I lean out to open the door. Now for the first time Jeanette Sue notices me.

"What are you doing here?"

"I came with Myrna. . . ."

"Oh, right."

She's looking me over, and then it's like a lightbulb goes off in her head. "How come you're not in a dress?"

She asks me the question, but her eyes sneak over to Myrna, who looks like she's going to throw up. I back up a little to get out of the way in case.

I sort of shrug. "I don't know. . . ." I don't want to see any more blood.

But Jeanette Sue is on to it. She turns to Joanne and says, "I love it! Do you believe Myrna? Is she the best?"

"Cool," Joanne jumps right in.

Are they weird or what?

And then to Myrna, "You're fab. I love it!"

And just like that, Myrna is back in and I'm out, even though I look like everybody else. I don't know how it happened, but it's like I'm the one in the red satin now. Obviously mean is queen here.

"Do you think your guy could drop me off. . . ," I whisper to Myrna. But she's floating in heaven, safe on the good side, and she needs me to stay so I can be the victim instead of her.

"I don't think so." She's all smiles and not a trace of tears.

"Hey," says Jeanette Sue, "come on, you have to stay, uh . . ."

"Twyla Gay." The totally recovered Myrna helps out.

"Twyla Gay! I love it! You gotta stay, right guys?" Jeanette Sue asks her people, and of course they all agree.

"Really cool," says Joanne.

And so, like in a nightmare where your feet weigh a hundred

33

pounds when you try to run away, I follow my new friends, dragging myself back into the house.

Myrna Fry

I can't believe that Jeanette Sue, leaving her party and coming all the way out there just to get me to come back. Is that a good friend or what? How could I think she was just being mean? I'm so ashamed of myself. But she loved what I did to Twyla Gay. She's so smart that she could tell the difference. I couldn't. Whatever. We're gonna have a great time with Twyla Gay at the party.

Twyla Gay

I have to go back into the party because except for Myrna I have no other way to get home. I can't exactly call a cab, I don't have that kind of money and I'm way too far from where I live to walk home. Besides, with all these people I should be able to lose myself in the crowd.

But Jeanette Sue makes sure that doesn't happen. She grabs me as soon as I get inside and drags me around to everyone, introducing me, purposely making a big thing about my name, which happens to be sort of Indian sounding, not that we're really Indian, it's just that my mother's best friend was. Normally I don't even care about the "Hey, you wanna meet Running Water?" jokes, but this feels hostile. And everyone is just breaking up too much. Worst of all, I'm standing there like a Myrna dummy letting it all happen.

This is the kind of thing where later you say, "Why didn't I just tell her she's a butthead, kick some ass, and walk away?" But you don't, especially if you're new and these are all the people you're going to have to be with for the next whole year and maybe more. So you tell yourself that in another couple of minutes it's going to stop, or that nobody's going to keep being that mean and it'll turn into a joke and everything will be okay. And even you'll laugh. But that's not what happens with these guys.

Plus you get one bully like Jeanette Sue, and it begins to catch on, and then even the little creeps are coming at me. Not really the guys. They just act like guys always do, it's the girls who are so way nasty. It's like they're threatened. They don't have to be, these guys look like real losers to me. Except maybe one or two. Anyway, all I want is not to be here.

There's beer all over the place, and no one is even trying to hide it. I didn't see any parents, so I guess they're out or in bed, whatever, they obviously don't care what's going on. Beer isn't the only thing they're giving out. I turn down grass twice and the punch is undrinkable, over the top with vodka or something like that, so I end up with a beer. And there's big tables of food, real food, I mean expensive stuff like shrimp and things, not just chips, but there's no way I can eat.

"Hey, that's not really your name, is it?" Some guy, a hunk type with streaked blond hair that's just the kind of too long I like, moves over to me. He's tall, maybe six two, so I have to look up. He's got very dark brown eyes that look sort of friendly. Friendlier than any of the others I've seen so far tonight. And he's smiling.

But I don't trust it. I don't trust any of these people. So I answer him with a kind of *Yeah, what of it?* tone, except I put it all in one word: "Right."

He gets the message and sort of backs off. "Hey, no offense, it's just a little unusual, that's all."

"What's yours? John? Joe? Bob?"

"Actually, it's Ryder."

"Look who's talking unusual."

"I was just checking Jeanette Sue wasn't just making it up. She can do that."

"That and a lot worse."

"Yeah, but she . . . forget it. How about we dance, Twyla Gay?" He moves toward me to put his arm around me, but I back off.

"No thanks," I say.

He looks very surprised. "How come?"

"Because it's probably a trick, that's how come. Find some other kick toy." And I walk away. I don't turn around, but I hear him trying to say how I'm wrong. He just wanted to dance. I don't look back.

I think he really did want to dance, but I can't take the chance. It's crazy, but it's like I'm in enemy territory.

I push through the crowd over to the drinks table and pick up a Coke, and just as I get it to my lips someone knocks my arm and half of it goes down my shirt. I look up and see it's Betty Jane Oborne, and she goes, "Hey, sorry about that," but I can tell from her smile "sorry" is total crap. She did it on purpose, I know she did from the way her friends are laughing. And the way she's, like, checking with Jeanette Sue.

I can't believe how I'm stuck here. It's like one time when I was about five and playing with the kid next door and we had an argument. A really bad one, and I wanted to go home, but she locked the door and I didn't know how to unlock it. I guess it wasn't that long before my mother came to get me, but it felt like forever, being trapped like that with someone who hated me. Now I have a whole party of people who hate me and I'm trapped here.

I should be really mad, like on the edge of exploding, but that's not what I feel. I feel hurt. All the way inside, in my heart, there goes the ten-year-old again. I can feel the tears lumping in my throat. I'm doing everything not to cry because that would be the worst.

I look for Myrna, which isn't easy when your eyes are all blurry with almost tears. I'm ready to beg her to let's go home, but she doesn't want to know me. If I don't keep watching her, she'll go without me. She could do that. I never want to see these creeps again.

But I'm going to have to. Monday morning. Still, I've got to get out of here now. The only thing I can think of is to wait outside in the driveway. At least then Myrna can't leave without me seeing her.

I go outside and sit down on the lawn where I can see the driveway. I wonder what my mother would think of her wonderful rich people now?

CHAPTER 6

Twyla Gay

Either I'm a great actress or my mother is totally dense. This morning, I gave her this big story about how last night's party was the most fabulous party I'd ever been to, and I did the whole house number, how big it was and all that. I don't understand, she's really smart, maybe not school smart, but she knows a lot and she's known me all my life, how come she couldn't tell I was making it up? I even named some of the boys I danced with, and then when she asked me again, I forgot half their names, but she didn't want to notice. It would have ruined her evening, because she was the one at the party last night, not me. You could see on her face how excited she was just to hear about it. I wanted to tell the truth to someone I could trust, but it would have been so mean to dump on her pleasure, so I made up more bullshit.

I swear I'll never be mean like those assholes. No matter what.

I guess maybe she's not so dense, or I'm letting it show too much. Now my mother keeps feeling my head, asking me if I'm okay. But I can't tell her the truth. I don't want her that far inside my life; she wouldn't understand. Or maybe I don't tell her because I'm so ashamed of how I acted. How wimpy and cowardly, almost like sucking up, I was.

This has been the worst weekend of my life. And I still have to do Monday. Maybe not. I'm old enough, I could quit school. Then they'd all win for sure.

Well, I'm not going to. Screw them all!

CHAPTER 7

Myrna Fry

It's the first time I can ever remember wishing the weekend would go faster. I couldn't wait for Monday morning. And now here it is and it's going to be totally awesome. Poor Twyla Gay.

Well, she shouldn't have been flirting with Jeanette Sue's boyfriend. When it comes to Ryder, J. S. is a total killer.

I got here a little early because I wanted to make sure I didn't end up stuck walking with Twyla Gay. She does have to pass my house on the way to school. I don't mind the half-hour wait because I can get to see the RCs when they get here, and then we can spend some hanging-out time together.

I'm dying to know what Jeanette Sue is planning for Twyla Gay. I hope she lets me help. I am the perfect one, since Twyla Gay thinks she's practically my best friend.

There they are! It's so funny that they all walk to school together. Will you look at Dawn Walker, other than that she's wildly rich (her father isn't just a lawyer for oil companies, he owns them), there's nothing really Ruling Class about her. She's not even as tall as me, and so what if she's a size four? And she's always going on about how she's petite. Like, how come she's not just short? I heard for a fact that she was going to be a midget, but they did some kind of operation and gave her some medicine to make her taller. I should tell Jeanette Sue about that. I mean, I don't think she would want an almost midget in our clique. Anyway, Dawn lives close to me and so does Betty Jane, so how come they end up walking with Jeanette Sue? And Anna Marie lives all the way over near the country club, which is the exact opposite direction. And they even walk home together, or at least they walk Jeanette Sue home. Maybe I'll suggest going with them today. We'll probably have a lot to talk about, what with the Twyla Gay thing.

"Hi!" They're still a block away, but I want them to see me, so I shout and wave, but they're so busy talking they don't see me. I start to walk toward them, and when I get almost up to them, I say hi again. This time they see me, but nobody says anything; it's like they're waiting for Jeanette Sue to speak.

"Hey, Red Satin, how you doin'?" That was Jeanette Sue.

"Great! What's happening with you-know-who?"

"I don't know who." Then she turns to her gang and asks them, "Do you know who, guys?"

They just shake their heads and shrug their shoulders like they mean *I don't know what she's talking about.*

I get it. Jeanette Sue wants to keep it secret just with

me, so I drop it and just ask regular nothing questions. Suddenly everyone is in a big hurry and they're practically running to the school, so they have no time to answer my questions.

Jeanette Sue and everybody go in through the front door. I'm following right behind.

"See ya later," Kathy Diggers goes, and lets the door slam shut just as I get there. And when I try to open it, my luck, it's stuck just like the back door the other day.

Worse luck. Here comes Twyla Gay and I don't even know what the plan is, so how am I supposed to know how to act?

"Hi, Myrna." She says it real soft, like she's afraid to bother me. She looks awful. Like she's got the flu or something.

I tell her hi and keep walking, but she's following me.

"Hey, Myrna. Look, I'm sorry about the other night, the party thing. I hope I didn't mess up your night."

"Hey, not mine. I had a great time. What about you?"

"It was okay, I guess. You know, it's hard when you're new and all. . . ."

"Whatever," I go, and turn and go in the other direction. I do it just to lose her, but she won't be lost.

"I mean, I would like to be friends and, you know, get to know the whole group."

"Hello. I don't think this is the time. Maybe next year, huh?"

"Okay. Well, I hope we can at least walk home sometimes together."

Oh, she's hopeless. She doesn't get it at all.

"Hey, we'll see, huh?" Like when my mother says, "We'll see," it means no. Get it, Twyla Gay?

"Okay, right . . . ," she goes, and turns back toward her class, which of course happens to be mine, too, but I let her go first. I don't want to be seen walking into class with that loser.

Jeanette Sue is going to have a picnic with her. I can't wait.

CHAPTER 8

Twyla Gay

I planned not even to bring up the party, in fact, I wasn't going to say anything to any of them, Myrna included. I was just going to stay away. Far away. Except I don't.

When I see Myrna outside the school I catch up with her and apologize to her for the party night. I don't know why, I just do.

I know it's really lame the way I'm acting, it's like I'm groveling, but I hate being stuck here all alone in Dallas, and except for my mother and my aunt and little cousins, I have no one to talk to. I mean, William is nice, but he's eight years old, and Annie is only five. That's not like real talking. And even with the grown-ups it's all about family and gossip about cousins and people I hardly know. The big topic is always about my aunt's in-laws. They are assholes, but I don't really care about them. At least not like my mom and her sister do.

Even though I planned to ignore Myrna, I don't. I can tell she wants to get rid of me, but for some dumb reason I just hang on. I even say something about being her friend. Just thinking about how I'm acting, I could throw up.

I swear I'm never going to talk to her again, and after that first little meeting I don't. I just pay no attention to her and walk right past her out of my first class and down the hall to my science class. I'm almost there when someone shouts behind me.

"Hey, Twyla Gay!" It's not Myrna, but unless I'm ready to pretend I'm deaf, I have to turn around. So I do.

It's Jeanette Sue standing there in her jodhpurs and boots. And she's waving and she's smiling and now she's practically running down the hall like she's going to hug me. I was going to ignore her, too, but now I don't know what to do.

"Hi." She's all out of breath. "I didn't even see you leave my party. So I wanted to know, like, did you have a good time?"

Her whole gang, all the RCs, are around her. It's like they're waiting to see what she's going to do. Me too, I'm waiting, except I'm dreading it. I only have a nanosecond to answer, but it's enough time to convince myself that maybe the other night was probably a mistake or I misunderstood or it really was just a harmless joke you play on new people. Even in such a short time as that I know I sound just like Myrna making excuses for those creeps. And I hate myself, but I go with the first thing, that I misunderstood, that she really wasn't being mean the other night, that I'm just too sensitive.

"So," she says, "did you?"

She's looking me right in the face and she's smiling like I'm her good friend and she sounds so sincere, so I say, "Yeah, great. Totally great."

"Terrific. So did Ryder. He told me you're so fun."

"Told me, too," Anna Marie butts in.

"Hey, look," I say, "I didn't know he was your boyfriend. Besides, all we did was talk for a second—"

"Hello. My boyfriend? No way. Not since a year, right, Joanne?"

"No way." Dumb Joanne shakes her head so overhard that her stringy red hair whips at her cheeks.

"In fact"—Jeanette Sue leans over and whispers in my ear—"I think he liked you."

The bell rings and I'm saved. Kids start tearing down the hall. I say I gotta go and turn to head into my classroom. But my luck, it's Jeanette Sue's class too, so she sticks with me and grabs the seat next to mine. Myrna, with the empty seat next to her that she's probably been saving for Jeanette Sue, looks like she's about to cry.

All through class Jeanette Sue is gabbing to me like I'm her best friend. In fact, the teacher tells us to cool it, even though I hardly say anything. What she's talking about is meeting tonight outside the Chinese takeout at the mall.

"You know that little place all the way down at the end of the mall?"

I tell her I know the place, but I don't really, except I want to go and I'm sure I'll find it.

"Everybody's going to be there. Even Ryder, and he's dying to see you. Only thing is we can't get there until eleven o'clock. Can you get out that late?"

My mother would have a fit if I went out so late on a school night by myself, so I figure I won't tell her. Or I'll make up some story. Whatever it takes, I'm going to be there. And Ryder. Wow! He is a hottie. And I got that he liked me, too. I could feel it, unless he was putting me on. God, it sucks how paranoid I'm beginning to sound.

So maybe I *was* wrong about Jeanette Sue. I'm not so sure about the others, but she's okay. I think I could like her.

Maybe my mother will get to see that house after all.

CHAPTER 9

Myrna Fry

I can't believe Jeanette Sue, the way she's acting so tight with Twyla Gay. I mean, I saved the seat next to me purposely for her. I'm too far away to hear what she's whispering about, but I think they're planning to meet or something. I heard someone say "mall." I can't believe they're not going to invite me.

As soon as the bell rings, I get over to Jeanette Sue and go, "So, what are we doing tonight?"

And she looks at me like she doesn't even know me and she goes, "I don't know what you're doing, but I'm busy with my friends."

Probably studying. They do a lot of work together, and I'm not in most of her classes. I must have been wrong about the mall. Looks like I'm stuck with Twyla Gay.

Twyla Gay

The head alpha girl just dumped Myrna. It was horrendous to see how her face practically fell way into her feet. If I liked her better, I would really feel sorry, but she's an asshole who has tried to screw me up more than once. Still, I don't feel good watching it.

I grab my things and shoot out of the classroom real fast. I don't want Myrna to ask me anything, because then I'll have to make up something and she'll know and her face will fall way more.

But she catches up to me.

"I'm probably not going to go with the RCs tonight, I have to hang around the house, so if you want, you can come over, but make sure you eat first. We're not running a restaurant, you know."

"Actually, I can't tonight."

"How come?"

If I were anything but a lame wimp, I would tell her the truth and watch her disintegrate, but I'm a nice guy, so I make up some story about how I have to go someplace with my mother.

"Whatever," she says, and turns to walk back in the wrong direction just so I don't see how upset she is. Who wouldn't be? Like I said, if she weren't such a shit, I wouldn't stand by and let this happen.

She'd do it to me in a heartbeat.

As soon as my last class is over, I shoot out the door.

I have to get home quick to do my homework and think of something inspired to tell my mother so I can get out tonight. Plus I have to wash my hair and think about what I'm going to wear. I may not have time for the homework.

CHAPTER 10

Twyla Gay

How come it can't be just an ordinary night where there's nothing special to do except homework and watch TV or listen to more of my aunt's mother-in-law stories? My luck, just tonight my cousins were invited to go free to this magician's show everybody is talking about, Renford the Magnificent. He makes some kind of huge animal disappear. My cousin William, he's been talking about this guy for weeks, and even Annie is excited, and she's only five. It's not like they would be able to go if it weren't free. Some guy who comes into the restaurant where my mother works gave her three tickets.

But someone has to take the kids, and my aunt can't because she works on Monday nights, and my mother is always so exhausted Monday nights because she does two shifts that day, so they figured I would take them.

Sometimes you do things you're so embarrassed and

ashamed about and you say, like, "How could I have done that?" And, "I'll never do anything like that again." But that's after you've made the mistake. This is before that I'm doing this totally gross thing. I'm lying and saying I have to study for a big test tonight and Myrna's going to help me. At her house.

I figure that I'll probably be out till at least one or so, and then I can sneak back in after everyone is asleep. My bedroom is on the first floor, so all I have to do is leave my window open and I've got it made.

Of course, if I can't take the kids, that means my mother will have to take them. She wouldn't let them be disappointed. She's also coming down with a cold on top of being really tired.

All this so I can be with the Ruling Class, a gang of alpha girls who really suck, and this guy who thinks he's so great but so far all he's been is a major asshole. I'm lying to my family, practically ruining everyone's evening, so I can be with a group of stuck-up buttheads.

Do I suck or what?

Okay, I guess I suck, but I swear I'll make it up to them, my family, I mean, but I really have to go tonight if I want to be part of something here. Okay, it's never going to be like Lubbock. Still, all I need is a couple of friends to hang with on the phone at night or IM. It would be a start, having someone to talk to in school, eat lunch with, or just hang out with.

I really think Jeanette Sue was sort of making space for me, and if I don't take it this time, maybe she won't ever offer it again. And like I said, she's really not too bad. I think.

Our house is so small that if someone sneezes on one end, everybody can hear it. I know my mother's not doing it on purpose, but you'd think she could take some of that stuff that stops the symptoms. All the while she's been getting dressed, she's been sneezing her head off. I gotta get out of this house, my conscience is killing me.

"Mom," I call out to her, "I'm gonna get an early start with Myrna. Okay?"

"Sure, honey. Do you want me to fix something for you?"

"That's okay, Mom, I'll grab a bite at Myrna's." And I'm out the door.

I find a place to wait across the street, behind some hedges so I can watch my mother and the kids when they leave. I plan to take William's bike, which is way small but better than walking. Then if someone has a car, maybe they'll give me a lift home and I can fit the bike in the trunk. Can you believe what I'm doing? It's like planning a bank heist.

After my mom and the kids leave, I hide the bike in the bushes outside my bedroom. Then I go in and start getting dressed and fixed up. It's going to take me a couple of hours to get myself ready, but I have enough time before they get home, which should be about ten thirty or so.

Since no one's home, I can blast the music, except for once I don't want to. I feel furtive, which is a nice way of saying sneaky and underhanded.

But that's not stopping me.

It's almost ten fifteen, and I'd better get out of here just in case my mom and the kids come back early.

William's bike is smaller than I thought. My knees are practically scraping my chin. I hope no one sees me. But of course they're not going to, since it's black outside tonight. Not even a moon, and some of the streets don't have lights. It's a good twenty-minute bike ride to the mall. I'm trying to pretend I'm back in Lubbock, where you know everyone and you don't have to be afraid of being out at night, but this is Dallas and it's scary. At least in my part of town, which isn't the best area. It's not a slum with drugs and all that, but it's got kind of run-down houses, and no one is on the street. I pedal fast.

After about fifteen minutes I'm into the HighlandPark section, where the houses are from really nice up to fabulous like Jeanette Sue's. The NorthPark Mall is about five minutes ahead. So far I have seen lots of cars, but no walking people. It's that kind of neighborhood where the people go every place in their cars. Even though this is a supposedly good neighborhood, I feel a little uncomfortable because no one is on the street and you get the feeling that no matter what happened, no one would open their door to help you.

I can see the mall, but most of it is dark, darker than usual. It's a Monday night and a lot of things are closed. The main shopping part closes at nine, and by ten thirty just a few restaurants are still open. I don't actually know the Chinese restaurant we're supposed to meet at, so I figure I'll stop into Maggiano's, a big Italian restaurant in the front, and ask them.

By the time I get to Maggiano's, they're about to close, but I can see someone in there. I tap on the door, and the guy cleaning the floor comes up to the window part but doesn't open the door.

"Do you know where the Chinese restaurant is?"

My luck, he doesn't speak English. "Dónde está el restaurante chino?" I ask him in my second-year Spanish. Surprisingly, he understands perfectly. And I can understand his answer perfectly.

In Spanish he says, "I dunno." And goes back to the mopping.

I still have almost a half hour, so I'll just ride around and find it myself. It won't be so hard, most everything else is closed.

And there isn't anyone around. I can't even remember why I'm doing this. Is it just Ryder? He's sort of a hunk, but I don't even know if he's a jerk. Or is it the idea of being friends with Jeanette Sue, someone I really have to talk myself into? God, am I lame.

When I finally see Neiman Marcus and Wyatt's and get to the far end of one side, I realize it's a much bigger mall than I thought. A whole lot bigger than in Lubbock, but then, everything in Dallas is bigger than in Lubbock.

It's dark and creepy, and I don't think William ever rode his bike as fast as I'm doing now. I'm beginning to hate this whole thing.

The restaurant is not on the west side or the back, which would be the north if this were the map in my bedroom. I saw most of the south side when I rode up, so my only chance is the east. And there it is, Hung Fat, squeezed between the closed linen shop and the closed Lord & Taylor.

And it's closed too.

My watch says ten to eleven. I've got two possibilities to choose from: Either they're not here yet, or those assholes have pulled a trick on me; they know the restaurant is closed and they're not coming.

It's seven minutes to eleven. I'll wait until five after and then just go home.

I try to sort of tuck myself into a corner of the building so I'm not so out there but I can still see if they come. There's a big parking lot right in front, empty except for one van way in the back. It's all banged up in the front and it doesn't look like it's useable. I hope no one is in it. But they wouldn't even know I was here. It's too dark to see anything against the building.

Still, it's so quiet.

Four more minutes to go and I'm out of here.

Three minutes.

Hey! Look at that! Lights!

They're here!

I'm a total jerk to think they wouldn't show up. I could have told if Jeanette Sue were putting me on. I'm no Myrna. I wish I didn't have the bike with me. It looks so dumb.

From here I can see it's a convertible. Maybe Ryder's. They're taking their time. Someone's standing up and waving. I can't see who. Must be Jeanette Sue. I guess she feels pretty bad that the restaurant is closed. It was sort of dumb of her, but I'm not going to make a big thing of it.

I wave back.

Move it!

Why are they creeping?

Jeanette Sue

I love it! She actually came!

"Wave, everybody!" I tell them, and we all stand up in the car and wave at her. And dummy, she waves back.

"See, butthead"—I poke Kathy Diggers with my elbow—"I told you she would come."

And Kathy blubbers in that whiny voice, "Oh, yeah, well, I didn't say she definitely wasn't going to come, I just said she probably—"

"Oh, shut up," I go, then I give them all my plan. "What we're going to do is just swing around real close, and when I say three, everybody shouts out, 'Hi!' And then we take off. Like, what do you think?"

"Cool," Joanne goes, and they all agree.

"Is that a bike she has with her?" I go.

And Maryanne Tobby goes, "Yeah, it's, like, a little kid's bike."

Maryanne is right. It's this little bike, like, for an eight-year-old. It's weird, strange, those kinds of people, it's like she isn't even embarrassed to ride around on something like that. Too much. Could she really think she could be my friend?

"Just let's do it and get out of here. She's making me sick."

Twyla Gay

It's hard to see exactly who's in the car or even whose car it is because of the headlights, but it's really jammed. Of course Jeanette Sue is there, and what's probably the usual gang, and from here it looks like a guy's head in the driver's seat, so it's probably Ryder driving. He has a convertible. I knew he was going to show. I could tell he liked me. You can always feel those things right away.

I would die to leave William's bike, but that's ridiculous; who's going to buy him a new one? I could make a joke of it. I mean, it is pretty funny.

They have their brights on. It's blinding. Now I really can't see. But I can hear them. They're yelling, "Hi! Hey, Twyla Gay! Hi!" and I shout back, "Hi!" and their headlights come straight at me, and then at the last minute the beams swoop around in a perfect U-turn, and with tires screeching, the car shoots off across the parking lot and out of sight.

The whole while I could hear them screaming and laughing. What an asshole I am!

I make Myrna look like a genius. This was all one big setup. I'm so furious I'm actually making growling noises. I call them every curse word I know. Out loud, too. Of course, nobody's around. . . .

Suddenly it looks very dark and emptier than before because now I know no one is coming. And being off-the-wall angry isn't enough to keep me from feeling scared. I grab the bike and start pedaling fast.

I'm not even halfway across the lot when the headlights on the beat-up van go on. I don't like that. But maybe they didn't see me.

I steer my bike sharp to the right, toward the other exit. I don't look behind, but I can hear the van starting up. And from the sound, it's coming in my direction.

I'm going as fast as I can, but the bike is too little to get any real speed. They're coming closer.

And then I'm in their headlights. They're pulling up alongside me. My heart is pounding in my chest from the exertion of riding the bike and just plain fear.

Thank God, they're passing me. They were probably just leaving too, but I'm so worked up that I thought they were coming after me.

As they pass, I see that it's one of those horrible beat-up vans with all the fenders smashed in and big patches of rust splashed all over the paint. It's like a nightmare car out of a horror movie. Boy, am I happy to see it go. Now I can just use my fury to power me home.

And then the van stops. Just about fifty feet up from me. The door opens, but I don't wait to see who comes out. I whip my handlebars around as hard as I can and, standing up, pedal like crazy.

I hear someone running behind me, shouting, "Wait up! Wait up!" and then the sound of the van revving up and tearing around. I hear it heading for me. The lights behind me are so close they're lighting up the road in front of me. There's no way I can make it to the exit before they do. I hear somebody running. It's more than one person, I can tell, and they're gaining on me.

All I can think of to do is head toward the buildings, where at least it's dark and the car can't get me. And I'm out of their headlights. Plus maybe there are places to hide.

I can hardly see where I'm going until I practically get right there. I almost hit a small stone wall that goes around a little pond. At the last second I jump off the bike, and it smashes into the wall and flies up and over into the water. I don't stay to watch, but I hear the splash. Right in the middle of everything I feel bad for William, but I don't stop running.

I duck into the little parklike space between the stores. There's enough light to see benches and cement pots holding big bushes. I hide behind one and wait. It's quiet. Maybe they gave up.

But they didn't. I see three figures coming around the corner. There's enough light from the car headlights to silhouette them. I can see they're guys, and big, too. Maybe even men.

They start looking around, checking behind the pots and the benches.

"Come on, sugar, we're gonna find you anyway. It's easier if you come to us."

"Otherwise, we're gonna get mean."

I feel like my breathing is so loud they're going to hear me. Besides, the way they're going through everything, like under and behind, there's no way they're not going to find me. I have to get out of here.

Twyla Gay

There's sort of what looks like an alleyway alongside a flower shop. I don't know if it's a cut-through or just a back door, but I have to try it.

I take off my shoes and stuff them in my pockets the best I can, then crouching real low behind a line of benches, I make my way over to the alley. It's maybe ten feet away, but I can't see down it, it's pitch black. I pray it's not a dead end.

The last few feet I have to stand up and run.

"There she is! C'mon!"

I dive into the blackness of the alley. I can hear them running across the little park.

Then I don't hear them.

I'm running down the alley, and it's longer than I expected. It keeps going. I keep one hand sliding along the wall just so I can stay going straight and not run into the wall. It's so dark I can't even see my hand.

I stop for an instant to listen. I would hear them if they were behind me. I heard them in the parking lot. They were wearing shoes, not sneakers. They're not kids.

It's silent. They're not there.

I slow down, but I'm still moving forward. Maybe the alley will let out at the other side of the mall, and then I can run into the trees. I saw a lot of green all around the back of the mall, almost like a little forest.

I think I see the opening up ahead. It's dark but lighter, not totally black. And it's not that far ahead.

I start to run, sliding my hands against the side walls, when suddenly the wall ends and I lose my balance and fall to my knees, hard. I can feel the cement scrape through my jeans. It's the first thought I've had besides terror.

Though I can't see anything, when I feel around, I can tell

there's an indentation in the wall, maybe a doorway or something.

It is a door, but when I find the handle, it's locked.

The exit up ahead is my only way out. I start to run toward it, when the outline of a figure moves across, blocking it. I stop and wait. Then it moves away.

I force myself to wait longer, but it doesn't come back. Slowly, carefully, one hand on each wall, I make my way toward the exit.

And then the figure appears again. This time it turns into the alleyway. "Hey, Hank! You there?" it calls.

And from the far end behind me someone answers, "Comin' in."

I'm trapped. They're going to find me. Panic is cutting my breath into gasps. Screaming won't help. There's no one here to hear me. Except them.

"Cut it out! Who you pushin'?" I can hear them arguing behind me. And then another voice says, "I was ahead of you." Weird, it's like they are on line for a movie or something. They're fighting about who's going to get to me first. I can't even let myself think what they're going to do to me.

The fear is so overwhelming that I feel like just sliding down to the ground and fainting into the safety of unconsciousness. But I don't know how you make yourself faint. Instead of woozy I feel so alive, like all my senses are screaming at me. I've never been so far from unconscious.

In the nanoseconds I'm thinking these things I realize I've lost the outline of the guy in front of me. He's disappeared into the darkness. I can hear him walking, though. He's moving slowly, probably holding on to the wall like I did. Now he's close enough so I can hear the sounds his clothes make when he moves.

I need that doorway. I slip back silently, trying not to touch the walls, then when I think I'm just about where the indentation was, I reach out and touch lightly with my fingertips. It's still wall.

I walk my fingers along until I reach the edge of the doorway. I back into it, flattening myself against the door. It's only about a foot deep but enough for me to be out of his way, unless he's sliding his hand against the wall too.

If he is, I'm better crouching down, but then when I do, my knees stick out more. I'm trying to decide if I should face the other way so that my knees are pressed against the door, which would take up less space, when I smell him.

It's some kind of, like, aftershave stuff and the oily smell of dirty hair. He's right there. It feels like he's standing right in front of me. I hold my breath. Seconds pass and he doesn't move. He just stands there.

I feel like my lungs are going to rip open, but still I don't breathe. A thick dizziness, just what I wanted, starts to fill my head, but still I don't breathe.

And he doesn't move.

He knows I'm here.

"Where the hell is she?" He's standing inches from me.

He doesn't know I'm here.

"How do I know?" someone from the other side answers.

"Can't see a fuckin' thing!"

"Just keep moving," says my guy, and that's what he does.

Right past me.

I give him the slow count of three and then I burst out of the doorway, my breath making a loud *aaahhh* sound, and race as fast as I can toward the exit.

I can't even hear if he's following me. He has to be.

Whatever. I run like they're all behind me, and shoot out of the alleyway and blindly keep going straight ahead.

I jump over a low wall, and when I land, I hear their shouts behind me. The trees are ahead of me, right behind a playground area. I tear into the playground, whipping around the seesaws, running between the swings to the far end. Right smack up against a high wire fence.

And they're still behind me. I'm trapped. The only way out is over the fence.

I don't even look up toward the top, I just grab on and start climbing. Without my shoes I can fit my feet into the little wire crisscrosses, at least my toes, and it's enough to grab on to and keep going. And it hurts enough to keep me going as fast as I can. But I can hear them shouting at me, feel their hands reaching up to pull me down, brushing at my feet but not getting a grip.

I'm afraid to look behind me, but I can tell from the feel of the fence that no one else is climbing. They can't get their feet into the small boxes.

When I think I'm high enough to be out of their grasp, I look down, and sure enough, they haven't started to climb. Instead they're running back to go around the fence. But I've got a good head start.

When I get to the top, I just swing over, and going down is really fast. In my life I never knew I could do this.

I jump down the last few feet, and without shoes it hurts. But I can barely feel the pain; I just go flying for the trees. It feels like I lost them, but then I hear them running and shouting at me. Now it's like a game for them. And I'm the prize.

Well, they're not going to get me. If I can just get to the other side of the woods, where the highway runs, with all the cars going by, they wouldn't dare attack me.

The woods are smaller than I thought, and quickly I see the headlights of cars and I burst through and I'm on the service road of the highway. I don't even hear them following me anymore.

I start running in the direction of my home. I'm sure they've given up, but I'm so leftover scared that I can't stop running. I still have one of my shoes, the other must have fallen out of my pocket, but nothing matters as long as I got away from them. Nothing like this ever happened to me before. You always hear "Run for your life," but most people never have to. It's the worst, scariest thing.

I think my leg is bleeding and I know my feet are all cut up, but I'm not even going to look at myself until I get home. If I look, it'll freak me out. I just have to get home. Except home is far, probably four or five miles. At least it's pavement for now, so it doesn't hurt so much. I'm really lucky I wore socks, so at least I have some protection for my feet.

I start to think about how much I hate Jeanette Sue and Ryder and all of them, and that makes me walk stronger.

When I look at my watch, I'm really surprised; it's not even twelve o'clock. I can't believe all that happened so quickly. It felt like the whole night.

It takes me nearly two hours of fast walking to get home. The whole house is dark. Everyone is sleeping. I left my window open, but my mother must have closed it, and I have to dig underneath to pry it open with a quarter so I can fit my fingers in. Quietly I push it up just enough to squeeze in.

I hold on to the chair next to the bed so that I can crawl in quietly. I do and let myself slide down to the floor. I don't know why, because I'm safely home, but all of a sudden I'm crying. All this time when it was really dangerous, I didn't cry, but now I can't stop. It's the kind of crying that doesn't make any noise except sniffling, so no one outside my room can hear.

When I stop crying enough, I quietly slip out of my room and down the hall into the bathroom. I turn on the light and look in the mirror. I'm shocked at how awful I look. My face is all red from crying and my cheeks are scratched up. I didn't even feel that happening. My jeans are torn, and I was right, my knee and the whole side of my leg on my calf are bleeding. Not horribly, just like when you fall down and scrape yourself, but it's really raw looking.

I wash up and put on Band-Aids and smear some anti-septic cream on my face. The worst part about how I am isn't what you can see. I don't think I've ever felt so unhappy ever before, and there have been a lot of times in my life when bad things happened to the family, but this time it's to me. And it hurts all over.

I hate Dallas and everyone in it except my family. And the people I hate most are in that school. I don't know how I'm going to go back there tomorrow morning.

Myrna Fry

CHAPTER 11

Everybody in school heard what happened last night. I mean about how Jeanette Sue, Maryanne Tobby, Kathy Diggers, Anna Marie, Dawn, and Joanne tricked Twyla Gay into waiting for them in the middle of the night at the mall. And Twyla Gay actually showed. I mean, is she a jerk or what? And then we, the RCs, all got to school extra early this morning and sneaked into all the girls' rooms and wrote on the walls and the mirrors with black markers, TWYLA IS GAY. Do you love that? Actually, I heard it was Anna Marie's idea. She's always talking about "fag" this and "fag" that. She thinks they all belong in jail. Anyway, Jeanette Sue called our whole gang last night to tell us, like, what to do. Actually, she was the only one who wasn't there this morning. Nobody said why. Whatever. And then we arranged to all be standing at the door that Twyla Gay uses so we could be first to greet her this morning. That was J. S.'s suggestion, too.

But Twyla Gay doesn't show. Finally the bell rings and we all have to go to our homerooms.

Everybody is really let down. I mean, we're dying to see her reaction to the stuff in the girls' rooms. She better get here by this afternoon, because once the teachers hear about the writing on the walls, there's going to be a big stink and the janitor will be washing it off. I suppose they're also going to want to know who wrote it. I'm not telling, and neither is anyone else in the RCs. One word and you're out. Then what?

Just when I'm thinking this could be bad for us, she shows. Twyla Gay practically sneaks into French class. I mean, she slips in so quietly that even the teacher doesn't notice. I only know because I'm turning around to tell Anna Marie something when I spot her in the back row, last seat next to the door. I can't believe how awful she looks. It's like her face is all scratched up on one side, and she looks like she's sort of trying to hide it with her hair. She's looking down, so she doesn't see me staring at her. I wish she would look up so I could smile or something. I'm dying to be the one to go into the girls' room with her first.

French class goes on forever. What a dumb language, like I'm ever going to get to use it. I mean, who speaks French today except the French, and they're a million miles away in their own stupid country? I was going to take Spanish, but my mother said it's déclassé and only poor people speak it, so now I'm stuck with this jerk teacher and she's probably going to give me a D because she hates me. I mean, it's natural you don't do the work if somebody hates you.

So what, all I care about now is going to the girls' room

with Twyla Gay. Just when I think I'm going to gag from Mme Leclerc, the bell rings.

I'm up and at Twyla Gay's desk even before she can get her stuff together.

"Hi," I go, "I was wondering where you were. We were waiting for you."

She doesn't even look at me, just keeps getting her books together. I can see her face is really a mess, and she's got her hair straight so it hangs down, but it still doesn't cover her cheek. At least she got rid of the curls. She probably got beaten at home. That's what they do, you know, families like hers. And worse. My stepfather, the asshole, had this guy working for him, and the word was that he got his own daughter pregnant. Is that disgusting or what? Actually, it turned out that he didn't have a daughter, but if he did, he probably would have made her pregnant; that's the kind of thing poor people do. Especially Mexicans and Laplanders. Most people don't know about the Laplanders, but I heard that one time from a Swede, and they would know. I think Twyla Gay is probably part Mexican. I can tell, even though she's got the blond hair. That could be from her mother, who's probably from Lapland. Maybe that's why her father hanged himself. Maybe he made her pregnant and that's why they had to leave Lubbock or wherever. I'm going to say something to Jeanette Sue because I think I'm right.

"I was waiting for you because I wanted to tell you something I heard," I go.

She looks up at me. I got her interested. But she still doesn't say anything. She's looking at me like she's trying to figure out what's up, like maybe I'm trying to trick her. *Hello,* she's right.

"Come on, I want to tell you privately," I go. "We got time before lunch. Let's go to the girls' room."

She still doesn't answer, but she's following me.

We pass a couple of the other RCs and I motion them behind my back to follow me. I wish I could find Jeanette Sue.

I look around and now there are four RCs behind me, heading for the girls' room.

Twyla Gay

I follow Myrna because I know she's dumb enough so I can get information out of her. And there's a lot of info I want now. For one thing, I want to know exactly who was involved in last night. I know Jeanette Sue, and probably the usual coterie, Maryanne for sure, Kathy Diggers certainly (she's so tall she always sticks out), Anna Marie, and maybe someone else like Joanne Wilson or Dawn Walker, but I don't know for sure. Of course Ryder was driving. Even though I couldn't see him, he had to be there. He does belong to Jeanette Sue. I'm certain that Myrna wasn't included. Not that she wouldn't have loved to be, but they love even more to exclude her.

I guess this all sounds more important than it is. So what am I going to do once I find out exactly who was in that car? I would love to have them all shot, but I guess that's out of the question even though it is Texas.

Myrna is practically jumping out of her skin, hopping around, looking behind, she can hardly control herself. Either something's going on, or she has to pee fast.

By the time we get to the girls' room, there are seven or eight girls behind us. Maryanne Tobby, Anna Marie, Kathy Diggers, Dawn, Betty Jane, Joanne Wilson, and a couple of other RCs. Something big is up.

The question is, Do I go in with them or what?

I stop at the door and turn around so that they'll all know I'm not fooled. And I'm not afraid. But I'm not stupid, either, so I tell Myrna I'll wait out here.

You'd think I just took away tickets to Coldplay, the look on her face.

"How come?" she wants to know.

"See you later." I turn to walk away, but suddenly I'm being pushed against the swinging door. Before I can grab on to anything to stop them, I'm through the door and into the bathroom. As soon as I am, they stop pushing and stand back, away from me.

I swing around and sort of crouch down and hunch up my shoulders like I'm going to run right through them. But from the way they're standing there, it's not like they're blocking the door or threatening me. They're just standing there watching me, their eyes darting around the walls. Anna Marie is almost drooling with anticipation. That's when it hits me. They're waiting for me to look around.

So I do.

That's when they scream laughing and run out the door.

It's all over the walls, the tiles, on the mirrors, and on the doors to the toilets. All the same thing: TWYLA IS GAY. Except on one of the doors someone scrawled TWYLA LOVES TACOS. It's weird because I do. And next to that is TWYLA LOVES DEENA. I haven't been here even two weeks, and already I know there's someone named Deena and I know her label: class slut. And I know something else, too—they're labeling me, deciding who I am. And it doesn't matter to them that it's not true. I hate the vicious way they've done it—splattered all over the walls in black marker, it's like an invasion, an attack. I feel like screaming and shouting

at them, but if I do, it's really over. And I know they're waiting outside the door for me. Waiting for me to come out crying like my inside ten-year-old is doing right now.

Really, what difference does it make anyhow, whether they see me crying or not? I'm finished anyway. No matter what I do or say, I'm never going to get out from under this. By now everybody's going to say I'm a lesbian even though I'm not. And even if I were, I still wouldn't want them in my private life.

All I have left is walking out of here not crying. And not saying anything. That's always strongest, when they don't know what you're thinking. Even if you're not really thinking anything except how much it hurts.

I wash my face, which looks awful from the scratches anyway, sort of fix my hair, count to thirteen (my lucky number, ha!), and shove the door open. My plan is to go left, and that's what I do. I see a splash of faces on my right, but I don't turn my head, I just keep going.

I don't have to look at them, but there's no way I can stop hearing them shouting about "How's your girlfriend?" "Are you doing it?" "Can we watch?" and all kinds of dumb stuff like that. Asshole creeps!

By now the hall is crowded with kids, some of them going to their next class and some to lunch. I see lots of them stopping and turning around to see the action. The action is me.

I can barely see where I'm going because I'm hurrying so much and I don't even really know these halls yet. And besides, I am crying. At least those disgusting girls back there don't know.

I can't believe how bad I feel over something so stupid as that. It's more than just feeling bad, it's feeling so alone. I

don't have a friend in the whole school. Except maybe my new girlfriend, Deena. But of course, I don't even know her. I haven't even seen her. Maybe I should try to find her. The slut and the lesbo.

Lunch is next, but there's no way I'm going into the lunchroom. And I'm certainly not going into the girls' room either. In fact, the only place I can feel safe is outside, and that's exactly where I go.

I push open a door, I don't even know where it goes, but it's okay, it turns out to lead to the football stadium, which is, because it's Dallas, huge, almost like a professional stadium. And I'm lucky, there's no one around. I start climbing the stairs and don't stop until I get to the top last row. I walk down to the very end and sit there, partly hidden by a pillar.

I'm not going to try to find Deena; in fact, I may not even go back to school. And I mean ever. I'm sixteen, I could quit.

I always hated the idea of leaving school and not getting to be anyone, having a life like my mother's, but I don't think I can do this. I mean, go back into that school. It's too hard and it's never going to be any better. Once they get you, that's it, you're finished. I've seen it happen. Even in Lubbock High they did things like this. I remember one girl, it was the slut thing. She was a senior when I was a freshman, and everyone said she did the whole football team. I guess I believed it. Maybe it was just like this thing with me. I don't know because I never asked, I just accepted it. I never called her any names or anything like that, but I just figured, *Yeah, she's a slut. It wasn't even like she was a real person, just a slut. Just like I'm gay.

The air is cool, but with the sun overhead it's warm enough to sit here without a sweater, which of course I left in the girls' room. That was the last thing I was thinking about.

71

But I'm not cold. Actually, there's something nice about just sitting here, alone. It all looks so neat and clean and well kept, I mean the stands and the grass on the field. It's really a pretty school. It would be so nice to be a part of it. Feel like it's mine. My high school.

I haven't been here long enough to know much about it, but I did see some things on the bulletin board that looked interesting. There was a note asking people if they wanted to try out for the newspaper. I'd like that. I've always loved English, and writing is my favorite part of it. Sometimes I write short stories, just for myself, but once I handed one in to my English teacher, and she really thought it was good and wanted to see more. That was at the end, just before we moved, so I never gave her any of the others.

There was a lot of extracurricular stuff on the board that looked really good. Light-years better than Lubbock. But I'm never going to get a chance to try them out. Even if I were to stay here, I could never join any of those things. They would make me feel too uncomfortable, the kids, I mean.

I hate that. I hate that those snarky creeps can tell me what to do with my life.

I guess if my family were different, rich and important, they could do something. But even if they were, I don't think I would tell them. It'd be like a baby running to her mommy. It all makes me feel so disgusting and weak, I just couldn't tell anyone.

I can see people down at the school door starting to come out with their lunch. Nobody's looking up here yet, but they will soon. I just have to get out of here without anyone seeing me. It's just this once, since I'm never coming back.

There must be a lot of exits all over, but this is the first time I've been in the stadium, so I only know the ones I can see from here, and they're both on the other side of the field. I can't walk across the field without everyone seeing me.

More and more people are coming out. I have to do it soon.

I start walking down the steps along the side of the seats. I'm about halfway down and no one has seen me. I'm watching the doors just when my nightmare comes through. Jeanette Sue and about six of her Ruling Class shitheads, including Myrna.

They've probably been looking for me.

I move farther over against the side, looking down between the seats. Maybe I can find an exit behind the stands. When I look back at the field, I see that they have spread out and are combing the stands like they're the police or something.

"There she is!"

I recognize Myrna's voice. And then they all start yelling for me.

"Hey, Twyla!"

"Come on down!"

I keep my eyes on the steps and just walk down, carefully. That's all I have to do is trip. Wouldn't they just love that.

"Hey, your friend's waiting for you!" That sounds like Jeanette Sue.

There she is, in the last row at the top, eating her lunch all by herself. Now I remember seeing her in the hall. She was the only one walking alone. An okay-looking girl, nothing very different—except in this school if you count being Latino as different, then she's very different. Even though about half of Dallas is made of mixed-up races—who can keep track?—you

I sneak a look down at them, and they're all pointing like crazy at the other side of the stands. And then I look over and I get the "tacos" thing. She has to be Deena and she's—surprise, surprise—Hispanic. Are they morons or what!

couldn't tell from this school. I don't know how they manage that, but they do. And Deena's got another problem—big breasts. I mean, not gigantic, just kind of big. And it shows. She was wearing a big T-shirt, but even then you can see it's a lot more filled out. Well, what's she supposed to do? Stay home? And whose business is it, anyway?

"Hey, Deena Lopez, your girlfriend's here!"

Deena doesn't look up.

Then some of the guys who were fooling around on the field start yelling up at Deena and me about how they want to watch, and all the stupid things guys talk about when they think they're being sexy or macho.

It's like Deena's deaf, she doesn't even move her head or turn away. She just sits there eating her sandwich like there's nobody else in the world.

That's going to be me. If I stay.

But I'm not. I'm outta here.

I get down to the bottom, but there are no exits nearby. I have to walk out from behind the seats and cross at least part of the field.

I could run. Or I can walk.

Without making up my mind, I start to walk toward the exit, and that makes me feel sort of brave, but just as I pass the last seat I see Ryder. He's with another guy. I recognize his friend from my English class. His name is Steve Dennis and he's pretty smart. I thought he was okay, but I guess if he's Ryder's friend, it's for sure he's not.

I kind of brace myself. I know they're going to make some smart-ass remark, which I've already decided I'm not going to take the chance to answer. I might lose it, I mean start the crying thing again.

Twyla Gay

But they don't say anything. I don't look up, so I don't know how they're looking at me. All I know is that they are definitely looking at me. I hate them both. Mostly Ryder for what he did to me last night.

I somehow get out of the ball field. I couldn't even say which door I used because I have this blur across my eyes that keeps my vision down to maybe a foot in front of me and only at eye level. I can see shadows on the sides, but nothing more than enough so that I don't run into a wall.

It kind of clears up when I hit the street, but then I'm looking through a waterfall. My own.

If this kind of pain were physical, I would be bleeding to death.

Myrna Fry

Jeanette Sue is furious that Twyla Gay went home. She had these fabulous things we were going to do. Like we were going to sort of trap her up on the stands. J. S. was taking one group, and Anna Marie was taking the other one, and we were going to go up the stairs from both sides so that we cut off Twyla Gay's escape.

I don't understand why J. S. stuck me with Anna Marie's people when I really belonged with hers. After all, I know Twyla Gay way better than anyone, and I could have helped. She probably wanted me to go with Anna Marie because she really needs the help more. I'm like a valuable second in command. J. S. really trusts me. We're very close. Anyway, it was fun seeing Twyla Gay running for the door. She didn't even know where it was. She was probably going to meet her lover. I wonder who it is?

Twyla Gay

I hear my mother in the kitchen. I didn't expect her to be home. I guess her cold is really bad. Probably worse from going out last night with William and Annie, thanks to me. I try to sneak into my room without her hearing.

"Twyla Gay! Is that you?"

I'm in my room, but I can't close the door, then she'll know something is really wrong, so I try to put on a normal face. My mind is racing around, frantically trying to grab on to some story of why I'm home from school in the middle of the day. There's a million lies sitting out there and I can't find one.

"Sugar, what are you doing home now?"

My mother is pretty in a delicate way, light yellow hair and really pale skin, except she has a kind of washed-out look. And she really does have the puffy, fluffy curls. And she likes them. And they look good on her. She sort of looks like light traces of what she must have been. She's got a picture of herself with her best friend, Anita, and they're both about seventeen. She looks so vibrant and happy, not like now. Now she looks tired and discouraged mostly, like a nice waitress, which of course is exactly what she is. And she's really nice. I've been to the diner where she works and everyone likes her. They'd have to, she's so gentle and she does a good job, probably because she likes the work. She never complains, so it must be all right.

It's no secret in the family that she quit high school because she was pregnant. With me. That's how come there is no father around. She told me that he was an older guy who didn't even live in Lubbock. Just passing through. That's when she gives me her warnings about not drinking, and if you do make a mistake, make certain he wears a condom.

I guess it's because she's had so little in her life that she's so fascinated by people who have all the things that she dreams about. Well, now she'll be able to relax a little because I'm quitting school and I can get a job and help with the money and she won't have to work as hard.

I don't even bother with the lie, I just go straight to the truth. Well, not the truth, but just my decision.

"I'm quitting school. I'm going to get a job and help out. Aunt Willa and everybody else will be happy about that, right?"

My mother looks stunned. It's what she wanted, why is she so surprised?

"What are you talking about?"

"I'm going to work. Help out, like you want."

"No way. Forget it."

"Hey, isn't that what everybody is always saying I should do? So we can have more money?"

My mother looks at me, hard and angry. No gentle there. And nothing washed out about her face now. "You're not quitting."

"Yes, I am. It's my decision. I'm sixteen. I'm old enough and I'm not going back."

"What happened?"

"Nothing."

"Nothing, huh? All these years you've been talking about college, and now suddenly you're giving it all up. Are you pregnant?"

"If you want to know, Mom, I'm still a virgin. How's that?"

"I want to know what happened at school today that makes you want to change your whole life."

I can't tell her, so I just shrug.

"Well then, I'll tell you."

It doesn't even sound like my mother. I hardly ever see her so . . . so determined. But it doesn't matter. I'm never going back to that school again.

"There is no way I'm going to let you screw up your life the way I did mine. Leaving school was the stupidest thing I ever did. If I'd had any courage, I'd have gone back no matter what people said. And in Lubbock that would have been a lot. Still, that's why it takes courage. But I was a coward, and now look at me. With the exception of you, I don't have a whole lot in my life."

"They would have made your life miserable. You'd have been stupid to go back there. Grandma said—"

"Stupid I never was. I was almost a straight-A student. Like you. But dumb, yeah. I could never see further than the weekend in front of me. And Grandma didn't help. I could feel how ashamed she was. Whatever the excuses, it's all history anyway; the point is that you're not going to make my mistakes."

"Nobody's making me quit school but me. It's what I want to do. I want to get a real job, make some money."

"I would say that somebody in school did something and scared you away. And now you're going to be a coward like your mother was."

I don't know what to say. I hate to lie to her, so I don't say anything.

She takes my hand. "Sweet girl, I'm not Grandma; there's nothing you can do that would make me ashamed of you. Tell me what happened and we'll find a way to work it out. But if it can't be worked out, you're just going to have to put your head down and charge right through. You'll see, courage is unbeatable, it will take you right through to the other side. And when you're there, you'll look back and feel good 'cause you didn't let anyone steal your life."

I don't think my mother ever talked to me like that before. Wow, it's like she's six feet tall and made of iron. And she's my mother, and she's on my side. I take a deep breath and try to think.

She takes me in her arms, and I hold her, too. "We'll do it. Together," she says.

I don't know if it's feeling my mother's love, or how safe I am in her arms, whatever it is, I tell her, "Okay, I'll stay. But I'm not ready to tell you everything."

"Is it dangerous? Because if it is, I have to know."

I shake my head no.

"All right. I'm here," she says, "and I'll wait."

When we look at each other, we see the big, fat tears rolling down our cheeks, and it's so silly that we smile. And then we laugh.

I don't know how I'm going to do it. But I know I'm going to do it.

Twyla Gay

I regretted agreeing to stay a million times last night, but it's different this morning.

I know how I'm going to do it. And I'm starting today.

Payback would be so delicious. It's probably impossible, but what have I got to lose by trying? My high school life here is totally over, I may as well go for it.

I'm going for it. No matter what it takes, I am devoting my life to revenge.

CHAPTER 14

Myrna Fry

I don't believe it. Twyla Gay actually came back to school this morning. She missed the first class, but made science, and I'll tell you, I swear she looks different, like sort of dykey, I mean really tough. Maybe Jeanette Sue was right about her being a lesbo. I'll bet she is. J. S. is very smart. Okay, she doesn't do so good in school, but that's 'cause she's busy running the RCs. You know there's a lot of us now. Maybe, like, fifteen counting me which makes it a big job.

It's not like a regular club that does messy hospital stuff with sick people, which can really be disgusting and take up a lot of time. Or boring things like other languages or community service, where you actually have to go down to where those people live. Ugh. No way. Besides, you know, poor people have a lot of weird bacteria that they're immune to because they grew up with it. Like leprosy. They don't get it, but people like us would and that's their plan. They're just waiting for us to get sick, and then they're going to move into our houses and take over. This kid who used to live next door told me that. And he told me something else, too. It's all a conspiracy. You know the moon landing thing? Well, we never landed on the moon. That was all done on the Galápagos Islands someplace in South America. It looks just like the moon because they all have black dirt from being volcanoes. And of course, Hollywood was in charge, and you know who runs Hollywood. Who cares anyway. It's not like I'm planning a trip to the moon. Right?

Anyway, we, the RCs, we mostly do . . . I don't know . . . things. People things. Like with Deena. Everybody knew she was doing the whole football team, but nobody but Jeanette Sue and the RCs had the courage to come out and say it. One look at Deena with her gigantic boobs and being an "Other" and all, and you just knew it had to be true. Rush Limbaugh said they did this study at Tufts University and they found that the bigger the bra size, the smaller the IQ. That's why she's so dumb. Well, she isn't exactly dumb in school, but outside it's like she has no friends, at least not the right kind of friends, so how smart can she be? If I were her, I'd change my name and pretend I was from, like, Kansas or Indiana, but then I guess I'd be Indian and that's not so good either. Maybe I'd just be vague and say France near Europe. That's far enough away from Texas so nobody knows what they look like.

Anyway, about what Jeanette Sue said—the slut thing— it wasn't easy because at first nobody was believing it. Even me. I wasn't with the RCs then, and Deena always seemed kind of regular. Hey, I know her from forever, like from kindergarten. Sometimes I would even forget she wasn't a real American like me, but then somebody would say wetback and I would go, hello, you're right, but still she was really popular in grade school 'cause she was so funny. I mean, she had this great personality and could really break you up.

I didn't even know she was that hot for the guys. But Jeanette Sue knew. She knows a lot about Hispanics because, like, her maid is one. So she really knew what she was talking about, and she kept saying how Deena was a slut until she turned the whole thing around and then everybody was so buying it. And now nobody would be caught dead even talking to Deena. Besides, she isn't even funny anymore. It's like she has no personality. She hardly ever even talks.

One time she asked me something and I just paid no attention. Turned out she was saying my skirt was caught on a nail. Okay, so it tore. Still, I'd rather have to walk around all day with a ripped, hanging skirt than have somebody see me talking to the school slut.

Science class is, like, weird today. Twyla Gay isn't sitting in the back like she usually does. She's right up front. And I could swear she smiled at me when she came in. Oh God, she's probably in love with me!

CHAPTER 15

Myrna Fry

The bell rings and I'm out of that science class way fast, and even though she's a lesbo, and you know how good they are at sports because of that extra chromosome that they have, still she can't catch me. I'm shooting down the halls and ducking into doorways, and I'm, like, way crazy to find Jeanette Sue and tell her Twyla Gay's coming on to me. And all the time I'm thinking about that night of the party, when we were alone in my car and all. I'm really lucky she didn't try anything. Probably because my driver was there. All along I could tell she was in love with me.

I look around and Twyla Gay's nowhere. I lost her. Actually, she's not even in my math class, so she really wouldn't be here. But Maryanne Tobby is. I could tell her. No, I'll save it for Jeanette Sue—after all, she is my close friend. Then I can be the first one to tell her, and she'll want to know everything about how Twyla Gay's putting the make on me.

"Hey, Myrna." It's Tammy Johnson, a black girl from my French class. How come all the losers are so hot for me?

"What?" I don't ask it like *What's up?* more like *What are you bothering me for?*

She hands me a note.

"Could you give this to Anna Marie?"

"No." Is she thinking I'm going to bother an RC just for some stupid note from a nobody like her?

Then she goes, "It's from Jeanette Sue."

Fab! I'm in the loop. Jeanette Sue to me to Anna Marie.

Anna Marie is late for class, so I have to wait until the bell rings before I can deliver J. S.'s note.

The class goes on forever. I don't even bother to listen. Like I'm ever going to use percentages or triangles or pi, whatever that is, or any of this dumb stuff. So instead I write out the names of all the people I wouldn't invite to my party if I were having a party.

"Myrna Fry." Out of the blue Mr. Webber is calling my name. "What are you doing?"

"I was just trying to figure out the problem on my own, like, you know, without your help so that if I had to do it, like, outside, I could."

"Whatever you're doing, put it away and do the work on the board."

He's always picking on me. I can never do anything right.

At last the class ends and I push my way up to Anna Marie.

"Hi," I go, but it's like she has this hearing problem.

Anyway, she doesn't have a seeing problem, so I hand her the note. "It's from Jeanette Sue."

She looks surprised, but she takes it.

I try to peek over her shoulder while she reads it, but she turns it away. I pretend I know what it says already.

"So, what do you think?" I go.

"I think you could, like, mind your own business," and like that, she's off down the hall.

"Right," I go, and give her an *I get it* smile.

I can't see her face, but I'm sure she's smiling. It's like this joke thing between us RCs. Jeanette Sue does it to me all the time.

CHAPTER 16

Twyla Gay

I'm in this perfect spot just outside the lunchroom. It's a small hallway off the entrance that leads to the supply closet. I'm waiting here. And I'm really nervous.

I can hear the kids in the lunchroom; it sounds like it's packed. I swear I watched, like, about maybe five hundred kids go past. Normally the first lunch period is about half that number, but by now the whole school has heard, and they're jammed in, waiting for me. I'm the show and the star. And in about five minutes I'm going to have to walk in there, right in front of everyone. You'd think they'd never seen a lesbian before.

I see Myrna coming down the hall and step back into the alcove, out of sight. She passes, so hot to get with her "friends" that she's practically running. She doesn't see me.

I check my pocket for the Krazy Glue. It's there. And the toy. Poor William. First I ruin his bike (which, of course, everyone except my mother thinks got stolen; I told her part of the truth), and now I've got his favorite magic trick. I'm going to save up and buy that kid the best new bike in the neighborhood.

I don't even know what the trick is supposed to do, but it's the perfect size, a little plastic circle that fits right in the palm of my hand. I've attached rubber bands around it so that I can slip it off my hand when I'm finished. I can, but she won't be able to.

Here I am, standing, ready and waiting. And I'm sweating. I sweat like everyone else, but normally you can't see it. This time my T-shirt has huge wet circles under my arms. Very attractive. That ought to add to the picture when I walk into the lunchroom. Or should I say "we"?

Where is she, anyway?

Myrna Fry

I never saw so many kids in the lunchroom, and nobody's even eating. We're all just waiting.

Naturally, I'm standing with my friends, the RCs—well, not exactly with them, because they're kind of squinched in on the other side of their lunch table and there just isn't room for anyone else. I tried, but Jeanette Sue just looked at me and said, "Pleeease . . . ," so I went back to the other side.

I'm certainly not rude enough to insist when someone is polite enough to say please.

I got stuck on line in the girls' room, so I don't actually know what we're going to do when Twyla Gay walks in.

Twyla Gay

What if she doesn't come?

Except . . . here she comes. And it's perfect; she's all by herself, just like the instructions on my note.

Twyla Gay

I smear on the Krazy Glue.

"Anna Marie?" I whisper to her just as she gets to the alcove. She looks around. I step out right in front of her. She nearly jumps out of her skin.

"What are you doing here? Where is Jeanette Sue?"

"In the lunchroom, waiting for us."

"Us? What are you talking about?" And she turns to shove open the door to the lunchroom.

I grab her by her arm. She twists and tries to pull away, but I hold on tight.

"Lemme go! What, are you nuts or something?"

She's furious, but I hang on. Then, with my other hand, the one with the plastic and the Krazy Glue smeared on it, I grab her hand and squeeze as hard as I can. She lets out a squeal like a cut pig and practically falls to her knees.

Myrna Fry

I can't see down the other end of the lunchroom, near the door, but something major's happening there. It's like all the kids down at that end totally stop talking and start making these way big "ooh" and "wow" sounds.

I'm on my tiptoes, but, like, I still can't see. Everyone is, like, jumping on the tables and chairs, trying to grab a look. I get up on a bench, but before I can see anything, some ass-hole pushes me down. And then some girl, like, loses her bal-ance and falls down and knocks her head on the leg of the table. Before she can get up to wipe off the blood, I jump up and take her place.

When I look way over on the other side of the room, I can see the top of what's gotta be Twyla Gay's head. I'd know that awful hair anywhere. And what looks like Anna Marie's streaky hair next to her. Weird. They look like they're together. From their heads it almost looks like they're walking side by side. Like, that's impossible.

But it's not!

They're not just walking together, they're holding hands!

Twyla Gay is sort of in the lead, but Anna Marie is, like, right there alongside her. Would you believe it! They're lovers! Anna Marie is a homo too. And she's the one who's always going on about how all gays should be in jail. Look at her! I mean, is she disgusting or what? Like, how come she never heard about "Don't ask, don't tell"?

And to think all this time she was an RC and we were, like, really close, sort of, well, she was with Jeanette Sue anyway.

I look over at Jeanette Sue and she's standing there, on the table, with her eyes popping out and her mouth hanging open.

Good-bye, Anna Marie.

And that's just what's happening.

"I told you! It's over!" Twyla Gay is really angry and trying to pull away, but Anna Marie won't let her. And you can see that Anna Marie is, like, heartbroken because her, like, lover is breaking up with her. Right in front of everyone. Twyla Gay walks right through the entire lunchroom and out the other door with Anna Marie still hanging on. The whole place explodes in total chatter.

I try to get over to Jeanette Sue to see what we're going to do, but before I can, she grabs her stuff and, with the RCs racing behind her, starts pushing her way through the crowds toward the door. Naturally, the opposite one from where Twyla Gay and Anna Marie left.

I squeeze my way through and end up behind Kathy

Diggers and Betty Jane just as Jeanette Sue hits the door. She shoves it open hard and it bangs against the wall, and they all shoot through, each one knocking it back. Kathy ducks through on someone else's knock back. I'm the last one, and the door is swinging toward me, but I grab it before it slams into my head.

"Hey, Kathy," I go, "what's up? What's happening?"

But she's running too fast to hear me.

Just as we hit the front hall corridor Anna Marie comes out of nowhere and steps right in front of Jeanette Sue, who has to stop or run her down. She probably wants to run her down, she's so pissed.

"You don't understand," Anna Marie goes, like, with tears running down her face, "I thought the note was from you . . ."

But Jeanette Sue has been so hurt by her betrayal that she doesn't even want to hear anything, so she pushes her out of the way. I feel exactly the same. But Anna Marie doesn't give up. She's, like, totally crazed trying to explain some dumb stuff about how she isn't really a lesbo but that Twyla Gay tricked her. And on and on with some stupid story about them being glued together. Like we should care if they're in love.

Jeanette Sue goes, "Shut up!" and puts her hand right on Anna Marie's chest and shoves her back against the wall. Hard. "Just keep away from me, you asshole lesbo!" she goes, and without even stopping to hear what Anna Marie's saying, charges down the hall.

We're, like, following J. S., and even from halfway down the hall we can hear Anna Marie crying like some dumb baby, gasping and sobbing, behind us. But we don't stop until we hit the front door. And then we just start to break up, laughing hysterically.

"I'm going across to get a soda," J. S. says, and everyone else, including me, goes, "Yeah, right, me too."

"Lose her," J. S. goes, pointing at me.

I get it right away. She wants me to stay here and see what's happening with Anna Marie. "Sure," I go, "I'll find out what's happening and meet you later."

And of course Joanne goes, "Cool."

"Like, a hundred years later," Betty Jane goes, checking with J. S. for her okay. Then J. S. laughs, and Kathy Diggers and Dawn and Joanne and Betty Jane start laughing. Me too. I laugh, which seems to make them laugh even harder. I love when I can make my friends laugh.

We all have a great time for a couple of minutes, and then they start heading across the lawn and I go back into school to see what's up. I can't wait for my history class this afternoon. Anna Marie is in it. And so is Twyla Gay.

I wish I could find them both right now, but they're probably down in the basement making out.

History is a total bomb-out. Anna Marie doesn't even show up. Twyla Gay is there, and she actually smiles at me like she did in science this morning, but, like, I'm not about to get caught talking to her, even though there are a million questions I'm dying to ask. Not for me, I mean, just to bring back to Jeanette Sue.

Twyla Gay

It was a brilliant plan and it worked perfectly. I don't know how Anna Marie is going to get that Krazy Glue off her hand and I don't care. She'll probably have to walk around with that little plastic piece stuck on her palm for years.

I hope so.

It was weird watching that scene when Anna Marie tried to explain to Jeanette Sue what happened. Actually, it was sickening, I mean watching her crying like that. I was right there in the hall, standing just behind the exhibition case with the Robert Earl Keen stuff in it. He's a country singer who comes from someplace around Dallas and he donated some music sheets, and they're crazy about him here, so they're displaying it right in the center of the hallway in a glass case just big enough for me to hide behind.

And I was close enough to see Anna Marie's face. It was awful. She was standing right under a ceiling light and her whole face was shining, all wet from her tears, and bright red. You could hardly understand what she was babbling, she was crying so hard. And Jeanette Sue just kept shoving her away. Even though I hate Anna Marie, I'd love to go up and give Jeanette Sue one big Lubbock-type shove and jam her right into the glass case. I can't stand that she can do whatever she wants like that. And she can because there's no one here to tell her she can't.

Up till now.

It was really weird, watching this happen. I don't think I ever did anything that made someone hurt that badly, anything on purpose, anyway. And all the time I was standing there, I knew I could have just walked down the hall and explained everything. Saved her. But I didn't.

And I won't ever.

They're mean and vicious, every one of them. And I, Twyla Gay Nobody, am going to stop them.

I'm keeping score: one drone down and four to go. And then the major enemy, Jeanette Sue. I plan to take her down together with that creep Ryder.

I wish it made me feel better. It's like a victory—I mean, I did win—so how come I feel so lousy and unhappy, too?

Lousy and unhappy, the perfect combination for running into Ryder. And there he is, with Steve again. I wish he didn't look so good. It's not especially his looks, which are really totally hot, it's this deceptive nice-guy aura about him. He's got this almost smile that plays around his mouth and makes him look like you could tell him things and he would understand and be warm and smart and make you feel good. Am I nuts or what? I can't even let myself think about him. It's really sick being attracted to your enemy.

"Hey, what's up?" Steve waves and smiles at me. Or is he laughing at me? I play it cool and just look back at both of them, no smile, nothing, just a kind of dead look. I can see Steve's smile withering away, like in slow motion, until it morphs into a kind of questioning look. Ryder never did let his smile happen, he just looks at me hard, almost staring.

"Like you don't know?" I say, and walk away before they can answer. I would love to look back, but I don't let myself.

Why are they pretending to be so friendly? Like they think I'm some kind of moron who's going to fall for that. I don't care about Steve, he's just a hanger-ona, but Ryder is the premiere asshole on my list, along with his vicious girlfriend bitch, Jeanette Sue.

He doesn't even know what really happened to me after he drove away. I would love to tell him right to his face, loud, so that everyone can hear, so he would know how I could have been raped or killed from their dumb trick.

I must be turning into some kind of jerk to think that any of these creeps would really care about me.

If only I could find a way to do them both at once, Ryder McQuaid and Jeanette Sue. Something that would really hurt, that would make their lives miserable, like they would totally hate getting up every morning, and all day long they would feel like somebody broke them in half. Just thinking about this is the best I've felt since I moved to Dallas. Only trouble is, how can someone like me, really a nobody, pay back the king and queen of the school?

I would do most anything, and I mean it. I would cheat and lie and steal. . . .

Maybe that's it. Steal. Steal Ryder right out from under Jeanette Sue's nose and then rub her face in it. Like they say, flaunt it, that's what I'd love to do, and when she's totally heartbroken and absolutely destroyed because some Lubbock hick like me has stolen her precious boyfiiend, then I'll dump Ryder in the meanest, cruelest way. I don't even know how, but I'd make sure it hurt like crazy. I can just see them both sitting on the side of the road (I don't know why they're on the side of the road, but it's a good picture), miserable, abandoned, and shivering.

I like the plan already. I feel like I have a purpose, it's like I have a fabulous new extracurricular activity with no teacher involved. But I can't screw up. You know how you hear revenge is a dish best served cold? And you think, *What's it got to do with food?* It just means that you wait, like when hot food cools off, you wait until it's cold and nobody is watching it because nobody wants cold food. That's when you hit with the revenge and catch everyone off guard. Got it?

It's been two days since that thing with the Chinese restaurant, and for me that's cold enough, I'm ready to start my second part of the revenge, so I swing around on my heel and head down the hall after my new love, Ryder McQuaid.

I start off walking with a big, warm smile, but by the time I hit the middle of the hall, it's sunk into my cheeks, turned into stiff, weird dents, so I drop it altogether and just look regular. I'm walking fast, so I catch up with Ryder and Steve just as they get to the door that leads out to the tennis courts. I wait until they go out and then run down to the door and shove it open, hard, with determination.

Right into Ryder's back.

I hear the *thud* and he goes flying. I didn't actually mean it to knock him like that. "Sorry," I say. But I didn't mean that, either. "You okay?"

"Yeah." He's not, but he says he is. It was a hard whack, and he has trouble getting up. Steve helps him.

Me, I'd like to kick him down again.

"You got a great arm there," he says to me, smiling through the pain.

I squeeze out a friendly sound, "Right." This is going to be harder than I thought. I hate this guy.

"You ripped your shirt in the back," Steve says to Ryder, and then to me, "Didn't I see you way back in the hall? How'd you catch up so fast?"

I think, *Asshole, Steve, mind your own business.* And I say the first thing that comes to my mind, "You dropped your pen. I was trying to catch you before you left school."

"My pen?" Steve says.

"No, I think it was yours, Ryder." *Ryder.* I kind of make it sound like it is about four syllables long. I feel like I'm playing a part in a movie. From the way he looks at me, maybe I'm not so bad at it.

He starts digging in his backpack, but he can't find his pen.

96

"Thanks." He puts out his hand for the pen.

I'm stuck. I have to give him my new Pilot pen that I love.

"I don't think that's mine," he says.

I start to put it back in my purse.

"But I'll take it 'cause I must have lost mine." And he takes my favorite pen. "See ya," he says, and they start to walk away.

Not a great start, but at least he is rubbing his back and sort of limping a little. They get about twenty feet away, when Ryder turns and says, "You feel like playing some tennis?"

This is fabulous. Marvelous. Great opportunity to get my plan started. Only one small, slightly horrendous problem: I have never even held a tennis racket. Why bother? Like somebody's ever going to invite me to the country club to play tennis? Tennis is so not Lubbock High. They would have said it was for sissies or some other stupid macho thing like that. But still, this is too good a chance to miss. I could just say I sprained my ankle or I can play only with my special racket. I like the racket thing better.

"I can't without my own racket. It's this grip thing. But I'd love to watch."

"Come on, then," Ryder says, and I walk fast to catch up. And then the three of us head over to the tennis courts.

Guess who's playing on the next court? Right. Jeanette Sue playing against Joanne Wilson. And just like in the movies, Jeanette Sue is great. And every time she makes a point, Joanne shouts out, "Cool!" All I ever hear that girl say is "cool." She's like some kind of agreeable moron, except I have to admit, she manages to say it different every time. It's like a talent.

Jeanette Sue is speeding balls back with thwacks that you

know have to come from the sweet part of the racket. See, I'm not a total moron when it comes to tennis. I watch the Opens too. Thank God I forgot to bring my special racket.

She must have caught me out of the corner of her eye, because she loses it for just a nanosecond, then recovers and practically jumps over the net and runs to Ryder. Kissy, kissy. And looking my way to make sure I see it.

I see it. And like they say, hard only makes it a greater challenge. I don't know why anyone would say that, easier challenges are definitely better. But for me, my mind is made up; there's no backing out now.

Ryder must tell her about me not having my racket, because Ms. Generosity offers immediately to lend me hers.

"I'd love a game with you, but I'm afraid you people are much better at sports than regular girls."

You people. Is that trailer-trash people? Bad-hair people? Cheap-clothes people? Or just plain lesbo people?

I lean over close to her and in a low, private voice, just for us, I say, "Lucky for you I'm having my racket restrung, or I'd probably kick your ass."

That's a combination of trailer trash and lesbo, and it really makes her eyes pop. I think I can give myself a point for that.

But that turns out to be my last point of the day. Jeanette Sue looks terrific and beats her opponent easily and then she and Ryder have a game and no one even notices when I sneak out. I don't know if I'm up to this greater challenge.

CHAPTER 17

Myrna Fry

There's a new Web site called Hilandparkslop and it's totally awesome. It's like you can say anything you want about anyone and it's anonymous. And I mean anything.

Can you picture what it's like to say anything you want about your mother, and I don't mean that she's annoying, everybody's mother is annoying, I mean like how she flirts with her own brother-in-law when she has a drink, or how she even tries to act real cute with the pool boy, and how her nose is too long and her eyes are too close together, and how her clothes are way too tight, and how she's the most embarrassing person who ever lived and I would even rather have Dawn Walker's mother, who is so fat you wouldn't believe it?

But the best thing about the Web page is that you can go nuts writing about people like Twyla Gay or, now, that lesbo Anna Marie. I don't think there's anything left to say about

Deena. But of course there's always Carmen Santos with the scar on her cheek and Regina whatever with the weird eye and that guy in the freshman class with a limp and Joyce Benyo, the fat girl in my science class, and on and on. Everybody has something you can make fun of, except of course the RCs.

All I do is punch in "Hilandparkslop" and there it is. It looks like everybody got to the message board before me.

HILANDPARKSLOP
Message Board
y do u think twyla gay pulls up the toylet seat?????

. . .

ha ha, u r 2 funny so did u no Deena an her do it in the grls rm . . .

pplz . . . she really scks . . .

yeah . . .

no i mean really . . .

ryder n steve say tg smells ugh . . .

u no she eets dogfood at home . . .

no y she left Lubbock . . .

i wan 2 no 2 . . .

babee . . .

n she got a sista hoos in jail . . .

her motha is a hore . . .

deena duz anna marie . . .

hoo cares . . . deena duz evy1 . . .

mirna is the biges sucup . . .

u r riteon . . .

That's not me, you know. I spell my name with a y, so that's a mistake, that really can't be me so it doesn't count.

There are tons of messages. A lot of them are about Deena, but that's such old news, who cares? I mean, slut, so? And there are a few things about Anna Marie and how she wears a dildo around the house, like when she's cleaning or something. And then there's more about Twyla Gay.

gotta get welfare girl, right . . .

hoo dat????

2yla ga . . .doncha no assh***???

duh . . . how . . .

com to club 1 7 saturday nite n c . . .

Club One Seven is a club for teens, like, with no drinking . . . ha, ha. I guess we're all going there Saturday night. Nobody said anything yet, but that's probably why they told me to look on the Web site. I got to find out what time.

Long as I'm here I get in a little something. Something small on Carmen Santos.

carmen is so greecy she can slide 2 school . . .

this is Carmen and whoever u r u can go 2 hell and u better hurry cuz if I find u I'll squash yor stupid head . . .

I turn my computer off fast before she can find out who I am. I call Jeanette Sue to find out what time Saturday night, but her sister goes, like, "She's not home." Weird, I thought she was an only child. So anyway, I'll go around eight or so. For something this good I can wait around.

When I sneak back on, the rest of the messages are, like, stuff about smelly armpits or dumbest (they got that Mirna person, not me, again), retard, biggest tits, will blow, and cheapest clothes. I put "Twyla Gay" next to every one of them.

Then there's messages from guys about who's got crabs or cellulite on the ass.

And then there's a whole page on weird and deformed. Don't you love that? That's like this kid in my English class whose right arm is sort of shorter than the other, and a new freshman who's deaf, plus there's the blind girl in the graduating class, but it would be a waste to put her name in, since she can't even see it.

Between Deena and Twyla Gay, and Anna Marie now too, they have practically all the pages. They even have some stuff for the parents, like welfare mothers and dirtiest house. Twyla's in there, too. Well, at least her mother is.

I can't wait to hear what happens when Twyla sees the page.

CHAPTER 18

Twyla Gay

In my French class everyone is suddenly very friendly. They all want to know if I saw the new Web site for Highland Park. And from the moron giggles of the RCs, it must be something really badass. Anna Marie hears it too, but she doesn't even look like she's listening. Ever since that thing in the lunchroom she barely looks at anyone, and when she does, it looks like there are tears ready to run down her face. Too bad.

I don't care.

And I don't even care that I don't care. They're bullies and monsters and someone has to stop them. And not by telling the teacher or your mommy; the only way is to use their methods and crush them.

Dawn is talking to Anna Marie, and for a second Anna Marie almost looks happy that an RC is paying attention to her, like she thinks she's in again. But then, Dawn's probably telling her about the Web site. I can only see the side of Anna Marie's face, but enough of it so I can watch the stretch of the smile line sliding back into her mouth and then drooping down toward her chin. She is so not happy.

The Web site is called Hilandparkslop. I can just imagine.

Now Anna Marie's crying again. She's trying to hide her face by doing the old nose blow, but nobody's fooled. Suddenly she jumps up, tells the teacher she's sick, and runs out of the room.

The RCs are loving it. While Mme Leclerc, the teacher, is busy writing on the blackboard, Kathy Diggers gets up and gives everyone the high sign.

Most of the RCs sit together, real tight, so all they have to do is lean over and they're having a meeting. It must be a great meeting because they're all hysterical laughing, silently, except for a couple of uncontrollable snorts, but Mme Leclerc is one of those dedicated teachers who loves her subject so much she forgets about the students.

The bell rings and I jump up, and I'm first out the door. I need time to figure this out. First thing I have to know is what's on that Web site. Know your enemy, right?

I shoot into the library and go right to Hilandparkslop, and there I am, star of the page. Deena is only a featured player, Anna Marie has maybe a walk-on, and Myrna gets a little mention, but knowing Myrna, she's so dumb she won't think it's about her because they spelled her name wrong. It's all pretty much garbage, but the thing about Club One Seven tomorrow night is very interesting. Very. Definitely a possibility.

But I'll need help. Maybe Anna Marie. But no, I can't trust her not to go running back to them even though they don't want her. I need someone totally on the other side who's been here a while and would know what's happening. Someone like Deena.

Only trouble is that Deena doesn't like me. Well, not me especially, she doesn't like anyone and I don't blame her. It must really be tough for her with all these vicious creeps dissing her all the time. Maybe if she understands that I'm going to take some of the heat off her, since I guess I'm set up to be the new Deena, she'll be more cooperative.

Even though a lot of the kids aren't with the RCs, most of them are afraid to be seen with me. Okay, so you're not in with the clique, still it's better if they don't notice you, and hanging around with me is going to make you, like, very noticed. So everyone keeps far away from me like I have the plague or something. Those creeps have the whole school scared.

I saw Deena eating her lunch in the bleachers on the football field the other day. She probably does that so that she doesn't have to face that gross lunchroom.

Ryder and Steve and some of the other guys are hanging out at the end of the hallway, so I go around the other way. I can only do one plan at a time, and that Web site thing is urgent right now. They're sure to get me in one of the afternoon classes.

I was right, Deena is up where she was the other day, near the top of the bleachers. It's a beautiful day, sunny and not too hot, and you can smell the jasmine. Too bad to waste a beautiful day in this ugly school with those disgusting people who only want to see you cry. Weird to be like that. I didn't even like it when my enemy cried. And I hate her. Maybe I'm just a wonderful person.

Wonderful person that I am, I start climbing the steps to where Deena the Slut is sitting all by herself. Like I'm so nice

I'm going to keep her company. From the look on her face I think she may try to push me down.

"Hi." I put on my best welcoming face, that's where I nod my head a little to the side, friendly like, and smile. It's wasted. She doesn't answer, just looks down at her book. But I can't afford to be sensitive. I need someone desperately.

"Deena the Slut?"

Now I have her attention. She looks up, stunned.

"I'm Twyla the Gay. Nice to meet you."

"What do you want?" She spits the words out of clenched teeth.

"Revenge. How about you?"

Her mouth actually drops, I mean, like, the lower jaw really goes down and her whole mouth is hanging open. And then she pulls herself together. "Yeah, right. Good luck."

"Did you hear about Anna Marie?" She doesn't say anything, but you have to live on Mars not to know what happened. So I don't bother telling her, I just say, "That was me." Even though she still doesn't respond, I can see that she's sort of impressed. It was pretty awesome. Ugly, mean, but she had it coming.

"I can use some help," I say, but she still doesn't answer. Well, I tried. If she wants to just keep taking it without fighting back, nothing I can do about it. "Okay. Then, I'll do it myself."

And I turn and start to walk away.

"Wait."

I turn and come back. Fast.

"Twyla the Gay. I really like that."

I can't believe it, she's smiling. And she's got a gorgeous

smile, full rosy lips that spread out across perfectly even teeth. And her eyes are totally fabulous, dark brown, almost black, and shiny. Everything, even her whole body, looks different. Mostly when I see her around, she looks sort of concave, like she is swallowing her breasts with her body, but now she's standing up straight; it's like she just woke up. Like when Sleeping Beauty gets kissed. Hey, what with me being a lesbian, this works perfectly.

And right away I know I like her.

I get right to it. "So, what's with the football team?"

"Actually, I only know the mascot. Hank, little guy with the red hair. He lives in my neighborhood."

"I thought so," I tell her. "And by the way, I'm not in love with Anna Marie, or anyone, for that matter. How about you?"

"In this school? I just about hate everyone."

"There are probably some good guys, we just have to find them. You want to help?"

"I don't know. . . ."

"Come on, Deena the S. Fight back!"

She smiles. "I never thought I'd think that was funny, but the way you say it . . . okay. I'm in."

She moves over on the bench and I sit down next to her. I did it. I made my first friend in Dallas. Now I start asking her about Club One Seven. And she tells me how it's at an outdoor mall way on the other side of HighlandPark. It's sponsored by *Teen Times* magazine and a local radio station. You have to be at least fifteen and no older than twenty-one, and there's no smoking or alcohol or food or even gum allowed. It's just a dancing place, and of course a meeting-cute-guys place. Maybe later for the cute guys, right now I want blood.

"Do you go there?" I ask her.

"Are you kidding? Well, actually, I went there a couple of

times about a year and a half ago, before all this. . . ." She gets that bad, unhappy face again.

"So, you think it's time to go back again?"

"I don't know. . . ."

"You can be my date."

And I know she's going to do it.

"I have to know every single thing about the place. Everything they do, I mean down to the last detail. Okay?"

And she tells me, and we spend the rest of lunch hour making plans for tomorrow night. I'm sort of surprised when she tells me that she has her own car and lives in HighlandPark. I figured she was sort of . . . you know, poor, like me.

Poor. I don't know why I, like, choke saying that word even to myself. Maybe there ought to be a better word for poor, and I don't mean *disadvantaged* or *underprivileged*, which is even worse. I don't want to be under anything. Under is awful: like underclass, underbelly, underachiever. . . . Maybe it should be something like *financially challenged*, except by now everyone knows what all those *challenged* things really mean. Personally, I like *nonmoneyed*. Like in, "Oh, the Starks? They're nonmoneyed, but nice people." I think that could catch on.

Anyway, I guess Deena is sort of rich. Nice to know that no matter how horrendous and cruel Jeanette Sue is, she doesn't discriminate. On an economic level, anyway.

I tell Deena where I live, and she says she can pick me up around eleven. It doesn't open until eleven and closes at one thirty.

It all sounded great when I was with Deena planning everything, but now, walking home alone, I think, *What are we*

Twyla Gay

doing? Like it's just the two of us against everyone. Well, I can't change my mind now, because I forgot to get Deena's telephone number, so there's no way to stop her picking me up tomorrow. I could pretend to be sick. I guess that's what's called courageously challenged.

CHAPTER 19

Myrna Fry

I'm going! I'm going to Club One Seven tomorrow night with Jeanette Sue! She invited me! And she's letting me pick up all the RCs. It means making two trips, but who cares? Actually, I'm not supposed to be driving kids at night, but my mother and stepfather are in L.A. this weekend, so they'll never know. If they did, they'd go crazy because they're always going on how I'm not insured to drive at night. Like I should care about insurance. Is that the most boring thing you can think of? It's not like I'm driving cross-country, all's I'm going is a big five miles away. Maybe a little more with the picking-up stuff.

Besides, I'm busy thinking about more exciting things happening, like that Twyla Gay and Deena are the big, totally hot new duo. Everyone is going how they saw them having lunch together today up in the bleachers. And in black studies—would you believe it's not an art class, all it is is about black people? Like I should care. It's not like I'm going to ever be black. Anyway, somebody said that they heard them talking about coming to the club Saturday night. Of course I right away told Jeanette Sue.

This time I totally listened, and I'm sure J. S. said we're all getting dressed up tonight, so I'm gonna wear my purple Donna Karan skirt with the matching Wet Seal top. It's my favorite, really silky and short with lots of middle showing. When I told Jeanette Sue what I was wearing, she goes, "Whatever." She's like that. She always says "Whatever," which is like saying "Anything you want to do is great with me." But just in case, maybe I'll lose the skirt and wear jeans.

Myrna Fry

So big deal, the jeans were wrong. They are all dressed up. Dawn is wearing her Donna Karan skirt, which isn't nearly as nice as mine and makes her stomach hang over. And Kathy Diggers, with her flat boobs, has got on last year's Dolce & Gabbana strapless, which looks really used and doesn't even go with her smoky eye makeup. Maryanne's silver bracelet is definitely not Tiffany, and I can tell her Coach bag is a knockoff too. And Betty Jane is dressed almost exactly like Jeanette Sue, except on her with her skinny legs it looks gross. But they all look totally great, I mean hey, look, they're my closest friends.

When I pick up Jeanette Sue, she's got on her Jimmy Choos. First thing she goes when she sees me is, "Hey, you deaf or something?" which of course shows she totally cares. I start to tell her how come I'm not dressed up, but she goes, "Whatever."

Like I said, whatever you want to do is great with her.

Now that we're really close, I ask her, "How come you're not going with Ryder? Like, is he sick or something?"

Kathy Diggers doesn't even give J. S. a chance to answer.

"Like it's any of your business."

"Do you believe her?" Dawn goes, and J. S. goes, "Yeah, like, he's dying."

"Sorry, I didn't know." I totally didn't. Usually you hear those things if someone is dying. But I didn't hear anything. I can see Jeanette Sue doesn't want to talk about it, because right away she changes the subject to Twyla Gay and Deena.

"Think they'll show?" she goes.

"I know for a fact they're coming." I don't really know, but I want to keep J. S.'s mind off Ryder. It works. All we talk about for the whole trip is how we're going to make sure nobody dances with Deena or Twyla Gay or talks to them, and maybe we could even corner them in the girls' room.

I drop J. S. and the gang off and go back to pick up Joanne, Sally Lynn Walker, Ashley Bauer, and another girl, named Janni, I don't even know. They're not important like the first group, my group. They're all in different parts of HighlandPark—I mean, I'm not about to pick up anyone out-side of our area—still, it takes us till almost eleven thirty before we get there.

When we do, they all jump out in front of the place, and so I park the car myself. Hey, it's not like I need help parking the car. I mean, only one person can drive, right? Besides, they can save a place for me on line.

I have to park way down at the end because it's really jammed tonight. By the time I get back, they're right at the door. I shout for them but they don't hear, and so they go in without me and I have to wait at the end of the line.

They make such a big deal at the door how you can't have cigarettes or alcohol or any kind of food and no gum. They even look through your bag, and just like in the airport they run that thing over your body. Once you get past the door, there's a little booth where you pay. It's like nothing, only twenty dollars. After you pay, they make you check your bag and your phone, and then you get a ticket, and they've got this weird rule that you're only allowed to get your bag one time before you leave, like if you have to make a call or get something out of it. I mean, like you're really going to walk around all night with a Tampax sticking out of your pocket. Like, it could fall out while you're dancing, and then you have to decide whether to pick it up or pretend it's not yours, and what if you need it? And probably no one actually saw me pick it up.

Even from the hallway I can hear Christina Aguilera. It's nearly impossible to find anyone when you first come in, it's so dark and crowded and the lights move around so fast it's hard to pick out people. They have a booth for the DJs and lots of other booths and seats and everything, but nobody sits in them. Mostly they're either dancing or hanging out drinking sodas and talking. The guys at the bar, like the bartenders, are around eighteen, and it's like they're stars or something, the way everyone is always coming on to them.

There are, like, a million kids and it's totally crazy to find anyone. I start pushing through the people, looking for my group. I'm scared I'll run into Twyla Gay and she's going to want to hang out with me. So far I don't see her.

But I do see Jeanette Sue, and she's dancing with Ryder. He looks really okay. I push through and start dancing with them, but I'm behind J. S., so she doesn't see me, but Ryder does and he smiles at me. You would never know he was so sick.

When Jeanette Sue turns around to see who he's smiling at, you'd think she was the one who was sick. I guess she's still feeling bad about Ryder. We have a great dance, the three of us, and we head off to the girls' room. Well, I didn't exactly know we were going there, but I followed J. S. and that's where we headed. But we never get there because just as we're passing the front door guess who comes in? Twyla Gay and Deena. Walking in just like they belong.

Wonder where Twyla Gay got the twenty dollars? Unless she's just pretending to be poor. Lots of poor people do that. You know, there was this hot dog stand near the school, and everyone said the guy who owned it was really a millionaire and only making out like he was poor so that his enemies couldn't find him and he could collect welfare. He was Italian, and you know how, like, they're all in the Mafia? Well, this guy was, like, a head guy, like he totally owned most of Las Vegas. He was pretty smart, for an Italian, because nobody ever found him. He's still there.

Jeanette Sue just stares at them for a minute, and then she goes, "Get everybody. We're meeting in the girls' room."

"Right," I go, and I walk right past Deena and Twyla Gay like they're not even there and head straight for Dawn, who's dancing with Ryder's friend Steve. And then I find Maryanne and all the rest of them. They're really surprised that I'm, like, in charge, and Kathy Diggers even goes, "Get lost," till I tell her that's what Jeanette Sue wants, then they're all, "Oh, my God, what's happening?" and all that. I don't tell them, I just go, "You'll see."

"Cool," Joanne goes.

And they all just totally drop everything and head for the girls' room. Me too.

Twyla Gay

We still haven't come up with the right plan. We have to check out the place and see what hits us. I tell Deena that I'll see what's happening on the other side of the dance floor and she can check out the girls' room.

"Right," she says, and heads right off to the bathroom. I feel like it's a military assignment and we have the advantage because they have no idea what we're planning. So far we don't either, but we know it's going to be an ambush.

Right in front of the dance floor is a platform like a stage with a huge screen on it with videos of the people dancing. The dance floor itself is jammed and really small for such a big crowd. You're talking maybe 150 kids, and mostly guys, so everyone is asking you to dance all the time. Just trying to get across the floor I get, like, six invitations to dance on the same song.

The music is mostly hip-hop, techno, and computer sounds with some classic rock thrown in. They play the big ones too, like Dave Matthews, J. Lo, Britney, Bon Jovi, Ashanti, and some rappers. So far there aren't any slow-dance songs.

The guys are dressed ordinary, but the alpha girls are really sexy looking, with microminiskirts more like big belts, and really revealing tops, like Bebe or Baby Phat two sizes too small, or tight black Victoria's Secret pants with Manolo Blahnik six-inch heels. You can pick out the queen girls because mostly they dance together in groups of three.

Like the three right in front of me. I'm watching this

not-so-gorgeous guy come up and start to dance with with one of them. How come he doesn't know he's never going to make it? This supergirl takes one look at him, and all she does is put her hand up to her face and sort of look the other way like he's not there. And it's like he's not. And he gets the message but there's no way out, so he's just stuck standing there, totally rejected, pretending to dance.

Then they do something else, too. A guy will come up behind a girl like he's going to ask her to dance, but she can't see him, so her friends will hold up fingers to rate him, and if it's too low, she just grabs her friends and goes off, I suppose to get a drink or something. The code is no secret. The guys get it. They see the fingers. Mostly anything under five doesn't make it.

But if they're really cute, like a nine or ten, then all three girls dance with him.

I don't see any of the RCs. I know they're here because I saw Myrna when I came in and she doesn't pee without Jeanette Sue.

Maybe we should have taken more time to plan this. I'm so busy looking around to see what's happening and what I can use that I don't even see that Ryder is right in front of me, dancing. With me. And there's no Jeanette Sue.

I smile at him and start dancing. Other guys try to cut in, but he eases them out. Even though it's not a slow dance, he cuts the beat in half and moves in close. I follow. He's not saying anything, but he's looking at me like I'm the only one around.

I force myself to look at him. It's not hard. The music is blasting, but all I hear is the beat. I don't really hear it as much as feel it. It's pounding right through my body. It's really hot in here and I feel like I'm wrapped in heat. We dance the whole number and neither of us says anything. Then Destiny's Child comes on, "Say My Name," and I wake up.

I've got work to do and it's not him. Not yet. I smile a thank-you and start to turn, when he reaches out to stop me.

"One more," he says, and I can see he really wants me to stay.

This is working. I'm not sure exactly who it's working for. I mean, it is part of my plan, but this is supposed to be revenge and it doesn't feel like that. I don't know what it feels like, but whatever it is, I have to take control. Without saying anything, I turn and head off the dance floor to look for Deena.

Myrna Fry

When we get to the girls' room, Deena is there and she's all alone, no Twyla Gay. She's standing at the mirror fixing her lip liner. Her lipstick and eye stuff are on the shelf in front of her. It's probably not even hers. You know how Mexicans like to steal. It's like my mother always goes how they'll steal the teeth right out of your mouth. Which is why they have such white teeth. Like, I'm not exactly sure how that works, but I know it's true. Well, whatever, when Deena sees us come in, she stops for a second and just stares at us in the mirror, and then like we weren't there, she goes on doing her lips. Sluts are like that, you know, they're kind of used to people watching them. Like the whole football team.

It's weird, she doesn't even look worried and, like, there are seven of us and one of her. Jeanette Sue motions to Dawn and Maryanne to stand at the door so she can't get out. Deena just keeps doing her lips. Then J. S., who is so cool, swoops up Deena's lipstick and stuff and, like it was nothing, flips them into the toilet. Deena doesn't even turn around. It's disgusting how she doesn't even care about her own things.

Now Jeanette Sue puts her hand out to me and I hand her her mini hair spray. I'm the only one who gets to carry J. S.'s stuff. Then she motions for everyone else to take theirs out.

Along with our lipsticks and eye shadows and liners, we always carry hair spray and perfume spray and breath spray in our pockets. So now we're all, like, standing there armed with our sprays aimed at Deena. Now she's beginning to pay attention. She turns around and looks right at Jeanette Sue, who is so brave she doesn't even move.

"Get out of my way," Deena goes, and makes a dash for the door. But before she can get there, Jeanette Sue starts spraying her and we all let loose and, like, without even being told, we're aiming right for her face, and she's covering it with her hands and putting her head down, trying to push through, but she can't because there are too many of us. Her hair is practically dripping from the sprays, and even us, we can hardly breathe from the fumes. But we're winning. We're paying her back. I can't remember what for, but it must have been something totally gross.

It's so exciting we must be screaming, because two of the security guards pull open the door, and we all stop dead like nothing is happening. Just as they come in like natural we all back off except Deena, who shoots out the door.

The guards want to know what was happening, and we go, like, "Nothing, just having some girl fun," and they go, "So keep it down, huh?" And they leave and we all get hysterical.

Maryanne goes, "*Hasta la vista, Deena.*" And we all start singing, "*Hasta la vista, Deena.*"

And then Jeanette Sue goes, "Now let's go get Twyla Gay, huh?"

And we all go, "Yeah," and charge out of the girls' room after her like we were an army. This is way the most fun I've had in forever. And like I'm her most trusted friend, J. S. gives me the job of finding Twyla Gay.

"What are you looking at, asshole? Go find your hick friend."

Twyla Gay

I'm about halfway to the girls' room when I see Deena running toward me. Even from here I can see she looks really upset. As she comes closer I see that she's a mess, her hair is all wet and she has blotches of stains all over her shirt. It's like she's been attacked.

"What happened?"

"They got me in the girls' room and sprayed me with everything. I can hardly breathe through all this stuff."

It's true, she reeks of perfume and hair spray, and I think I even smell some breath spray I take her arm and lead her over to the quieter side behind the bar, where the empty booths are. People look at us as we pass, but nobody really cares enough to stop dancing or flirting. I pass a table and grab a napkin so she can dry her hair and her face.

We sit down in one of the booths and she tells me what they did. It's all I can do to just sit there and listen, all I want to do is rip that bitch Jeanette Sue apart. Deena keeps holding me down.

"Ambush. Remember ambush? We have to outsmart them," she says.

"How about just punch her in the mouth?"

"Unrealistic."

"So then what?"

"I don't know."

And neither do I. "It's over. We lost."

"No way," says Deena.

I had to convince her to fight back, and now she's the one who's convincing me. "Think," she says. "Think the meanest you can."

I'm thinking, but it's very hard to be mean on command. I can think of a million ways to torture Jeanette Sue, all of them when I'm in my bed at night, but now I haven't got one thought. But I'm trying.

And then, just like that, I see it.

Right on the bar.

There's this thing they do, the bouncers. They choose three girls, always the real alpha girls, I mean like the stars of the whole place. Right now it's three girls I don't know, but they fit the bill perfectly, the right boots with stick heels, skin-tight black pants, and sparkle tube tops, and they're dancing their booties off.

"Did they get your lip gloss?" I ask Deena, and she says no.

"Great," I say, and dig in my pocket for mine.

"What's up?"

"I have an idea. Wanna hear?"

Myrna Fry

I'm so dying to see Deena, but I can't find her. Like, she must have gone home. But Twyla Gay is still here, standing at the bar and having this long conversation with one of the bouncers, and she's doing all this smiling and flirting and practically dancing with him. And he's so liking it. And then she kind of gives him a little wiggle of her fingers and walks away.

But obviously he didn't like her that much because he's heading right over to Jeanette Sue. I push through the crowd to get close enough so I can know what's happening.

Cool. He's choosing us to dance on the bar. Well, Jeanette Sue, anyway, and she'll probably do me and maybe Maryanne or Dawn. Dawn's a pretty good dancer and I'm better than Maryanne, so it will probably be us three. They always have three girls doing it.

Like I said, she chooses Dawn and then she looks around, but I'm the only RC there, so I offer, "I can do it."

"You kidding?" she goes, and then she sees Joanne Wilson way over on the other side and she's, like, waving frantically to her. Then Joanne sees her and comes running over. And she goes, "Hey, you're gonna dance. Get ready."

"Cool!" Joanne is practically, like, jumping up and down. And the three of them start fixing their hair and all. J. S. hands me her makeup, and then they all hand me their stuff to hold and start pushing through the crowd to get to the bar.

Do you believe how I ruined that? All because she thought I was kidding around. Like, I was so totally serious, but how was she going to know?

Deena's still here, because I can see her and Twyla Gay way down at the end of the bar. Wait till they find out that Jeanette Sue is gonna dance.

The way they're hanging over the bar halfway up and practically crawling all over it, they probably think that's how they'll get noticed. Yeah, fat chance. I don't know why they bother to stick around, like anybody ever is going to choose them to dance. They must guess that, because now they're moving away from the bar, going way in the back, where they belong.

They're playing Jeanette Sue's favorite CD, *Touch Me*. It's her request. Kathy Diggers said that J. S. made up a special dance to go with this song in case she has to audition for a show. Wait till they see her dance, I mean, it's not just like some regular dancing. She really choreographs her stuff. She's planning to be a hip-hop dancer.

Now everyone is crowding around the bar waiting for our three RCs to get up. Ryder and Steve and some guys from Wenton Boys, which is a prep school on the other side of Dallas. J. S. is always talking about how cute those guys are. Wait till they see how totally amazing she is. She's so going to have all of them going crazy for her.

They do it the same way all the time, the bar thing. The three girls start down at the opposite end of the bar and dance their way up to the round part, where Twyla Gay and Deena were hanging around, and that's where they really let go.

From here I can see the bouncers fighting over who's going to help Jeanette Sue up on the bar. One of them is so really good-looking, and that's the one J. S. lets lift her up. As soon as all three are up, they shine, like, this big spotlight on them and they start dancing down the bar.

Twyla Gay

Deena and I are way in the back now, but we can totally see everything. Jeanette Sue and her creep snarkies are getting up on the bar. She acts like she's a real star doing this dance routine that looks like she lifted it straight out of J. Lo. Dawn and Joanne are like her backups, but it's like Jeanette Sue is alone on stage, the way she keeps hogging the spotlight and flinging her arms, practically knocking them in their faces. She's probably pretty good, but I hate her so much she looks disgusting to me.

Now all three are beginning to work their way down to the end of the bar. Deena is pinching my arm and kind of jumping up and down a little. Me too, I'm getting excited. And a little scared. I'm not worried that it won't work, I'm worried that it will work too well. So, nobody said revenge was pretty.

Now they're halfway down to the round part of the bar, dancing their booties off. Really getting going and a lot of people are watching. Just what we want.

Jeanette Sue

"Kiss me on the neck
And whisper in my ear
All the perfect words
That can take me."

The spotlight is on me. No matter where I move, it sticks with me. It loves me. And even though I can't see them, I know everyone is watching me. Everyone is always watching me. That's the way it is when you're beautiful. It's not like I'm conceited. It's not my fault everyone says I'm the most beautiful girl in the school. So I guess I am.

I love the way the light blinds me. I can't see anything out there except blotches of moving darkness. I feel like I'm shining. Dazzling. Hot. And it makes the music so totally intense. It's like I don't even know that anyone else is there. Besides, no one is watching them anyway. Only me.

Even J. Lo doesn't move the way I do. And I don't even have to try. It comes naturally. I hope that Twyla Gay is watching.

No way that washed-out little trailer trash has got a chance with Ryder.

"Just like an angel
Who spread her wings
I'll fly over innocence
On my way to anything."

Oooh, I love this part. Watch me! Watch me!

"Ain't no doubt about it
I don't want to go without it."

I'm saving my big move for the round part of the bar at the end. I'm almost there.

Dawn and Joanne keep getting in my way. "Get back," I go, and they jump back out of the spotlight.

Now it's all mine. I'm like the solo act, with them kind of keeping time in the back. I motion to them to stay on either side of me when we get down the end of the bar so I can have room to do my big finale leap.

"Come on baby,
Touch me
Touch me where it counts."

Look at me! Look at me! Arms way out, wiggling down, tossing the hair, twisting the shoulders, knees bending, and up for the leap. . . .
Wheeee . . . I'm flying!
Oh, my God! Help me! I'm flying. . . .

**Twyla Gay
Oh, my God! She's flying!**

"Look at her!" I poke Deena.

Everyone is shouting, "Yeah! Go, girl!" And Jeanette Sue is going! She's sliding off the bar, sailing in midair, her legs and arms spread wide. Not the pretty kind of wide either. She looks like a flying dog. And the joker on the spotlight keeps it following her. She's about ten feet out when some guys grab her so she doesn't smash into the wall. Guess we didn't think of that. But anyway, she's not hurt, just totally embarrassed.

Meanwhile, Dawn and Joanne are sliding all over the bar like they're skating on lip gloss, which of course they are. For a couple of seconds it's all really smooth and nice, until *bam*, they slam into each other. And then go *splat*, right on their booties, with their legs shooting up and their skirts up around their necks. We couldn't be luckier. They've both got on the worst underwear. Dawn's look like something she got when she was five, with little bunnies, and Joanne's are definitely period pants, you know, old and ugly, specially saved so you don't ruin your good thongs.

I don't know who starts it, it wasn't us, though I wish it was, but someone begins to laugh and then it catches on and everyone is hysterical, falling down, and Jeanette Sue is so embarrassed that she starts to cry and runs out. Of course Dawn and Joanne are right behind her.

"We did it!" Deena says to me, and we give each other a high five.

"Teach her to mess around with us."

"And all it cost were two lip glosses. You are brilliant."

"Thank you," I say, "and you are one of the best lip gloss smearers around."

In two seconds all the rest of the RCs follow their leader out, and now we can really have a good time.

"What happened?" The girl next to us wants to know. Before I can answer, Tammy Johnson from our school jumps in, "I heard that they cleaned the bar with furniture polish."

"I mean, how dumb is that?" I say.

"Yeah, right," Deena says.

"Did you see those underpants?" Tammy says, and you can see she's really loving this. Tammy is just the kind of girl Jeanette Sue would hate. She's just too smart for her. On top of that she has the nerve to be African American and proud of it. That must make Jeanette Sue really nuts.

Now the three of us are reliving the whole thing, and then two other girls, Sally Lynn Walker and Ashley Bauer, sort of fringe RC wanna-bees who were standing by, get into it and we're all having a great time. It's like we've overthrown the tyrant and now everybody's getting up the courage to say anything they want.

And now the music starts up again and we all start dancing, and I'm having the best time I've had since I moved to Dallas.

CHAPTER 21

Twyla Gay

I got my first IM ever from my first friend in Dallas. Deena sent it this morning. Or maybe she sent it last night after we got home. All it said was "Are we wicked or what?" and then another from her, "Dawn and Joanne got dumped by the RCs. Jeanette Sue probably didn't want any reminders of last night."

And then a third IM: "Meeting of the Revenge Committee, twelve o'clock, Monday, seventh row, football stadium. Bring a friend. Undesirable and bloodthirsty preferred. Signed, Deena the S."

Luckily there are lots of undesirables. According to the Ruling Class, like, just about the whole school. But we have to organize them and that's going to be tough. They're scared. The RCs are powerful, popular, rich, and really nasty. We have to think of them sort of like a political party in power that we have to overthrow.

Yeah, we got lucky last night, but we're never going to really win with just the two of us. This is a revolution. We need the mob!

I make a list of the most undesirable kids, like Deena and me. After six pages I realize that I can have my choice of just about anyone in the whole school.

I figure I'll start with Carmen Santos. She sounded tough on the e-mail.

I look her up in the phone book and there are, like, a million Santoses, but luckily she has her own phone. I thought she would live around me, but she doesn't. She lives in HighlandPark. See that? Just 'cause she's Hispanic, I figured she was poor. Whoops, I mean nonmoneyed. Gotta watch that, lumping people according to labels. It's like Vickery house—white trash.

I call Carmen. It's sort of awkward on the phone and she's not so friendly.

"I was just wondering, how do you feel about Jeanette Sue?" I start off.

"Why do you want to know?"

"I think she's a bully, an asshole, and a butthead."

"Is this some kind of test?"

"No."

"Are you thinking about me for the RCs? Is that why you're asking me all this?"

"No, I hate the RCs."

"Come off it. You're looking to invite me in, right? And you want to make sure I'm good material, right? Well, I so think Jeanette Sue is, like, way totally great, and I would do anything to be in the RCs. And the only reason I have a Spanish name is because my father, who isn't even really my father, had to do it for tax reasons, and I—"

I hang up.

Deena calls me, and her story is even worse. She called Charlotte Whitehead, who practically got hysterical, I mean really crying scared, and said not to ever call her again and if she told anyone that they spoke on the phone, she was going to report her for being a stalker.

I try Linda Torrey, but she hangs up as soon as she hears my name. It's a little better with Tammy Johnson, she agrees Jeanette Sue is evil, but she's not going to risk her whole high school life just for what, justice?

"Are you kidding?" she says. "There's no justice in high school. All you can do is try to stay out of their way."

We try seven other kids, but they're all chicken. Deena says there's a girl named Elizabeth King who used to be friends with the RCs, but they dumped her. The awful thing is that everyone knows but her. She keeps chasing them, which is weird because she's so much nicer and smarter than they are. How come she keeps going back for more? Maybe we should talk to her.

Deena and I decide we have to get to these people face-to-face. We tell everyone that there is a meeting at lunchtime tomorrow, out back in the stadium.

Whatever happens tomorrow, whoever shows up, it's still got to be a fabulous day. We destroyed the queen. Long live the nobodies!

Deena and I are breaking up on the phone talking about the flying dog. "Maybe Jeanette Sue won't even show up," I say.

"You mean Captain Underpants?"

"I love it!"

"I'm spreading it first thing tomorrow."

"She's going to be groveling at our feet."

Twyla Gay

CHAPTER 22

This is the first day since I got here that I feel kind of happy, sort of like maybe I belong? Like this is really going to be my school. In fact, I can't wait to get there to enjoy Saturday night's triumph, so I leave extra early, and when I hit the HighlandPark neighborhood, I see Ashley Bauer and that girl Janni something from the other night. And you know what? They wait up for me.

Does that sound like my inside ten-year-old or what? Big deal, so they wait up for me. Really lame how much I like it. I'm glad nobody knows.

Of course, they also don't know about Deena and me setting it all up. I feel a little weird about what we did. It was, like, totally brutal. So was the thing with Anna Marie. Very Jeanette Sue. But still, it was nothing like what they did to me at the mall. I've got to keep saying that to myself.

But it's so not just revenge, as yummy as that is, it's more. It's cosmic. I look at it like I'm making the world safe for all the nerds, geeks, and other nons—the nonmoneyed, the nonthin, the nonchic—in other words, except for the cheerleaders, the rest of us.

And I'm doing it my way.

Ashley and Janni think it's okay. We have a great time walking to school. I mean, we're breaking up about the flying dog bit. Thanks to me, J. S. will formally be known as Captain Underpants. They love it and I know it's going to be all over the school by lunch. I tell them about the meeting today at noon in the football stadium and they, like, sort of hesitate for a second, but then they both say, "Yeah, great idea."

I can't wait for everyone to see Jeanette Sue groveling.

From a block down I can see a group of girls on the front steps of the school. As we get closer I see it's the whole Ruling Class minus Joanne and Dawn. Jeanette Sue is smack in the middle.

And she's not groveling. In fact, she's got her army standing in a line blocking the door, waiting for me. The only other one missing is Anna Marie. Even Myrna is there. Of course, they squeezed her so far down at the end that she has to hang on to the brick wall just so she doesn't fall off the entrance platform.

And my new friends, Ashley and Janni? I look around. Gone. Disappeared like in a magic show. I can't even figure how they did that so fast.

And Jeanette Sue? It's like she's totally undefeated. Standing there in her jodhpurs and boots, all she needs is the whip, and with the sun dazzling her hair, sparkling her wet-shine lipstick, the whole thing makes her look like she's in a spotlight. Like some great force is with her.

Maybe I'm on the wrong side.

Now she steps out from the line, and I swear the sun follows her. She turns and looks at her troops and then right at me. She comes down one step.

"It wasn't furniture polish," she says, "it was lip gloss."

I shrug my shoulders, but I don't say anything.

"Tom Devons saw and heard."

And then she comes down the other two steps and she's practically in my face. She's terrifying and she doesn't have even one zit.

"You're finished here, bitch."

That was her, not me. I still don't say a word. I'm going on the silence-is-scary thing. Yeah, maybe if you're carrying a sledgehammer it is, but there's no way Jeanette Sue Krumholz looks scared now. Probably because there's no scared left, I've got it all myself.

And then, like it's some army maneuver, J. S. steps back and all the rest of them come down the steps and surround me.

But all they do is just bump into me. Like each one sort of bumps me. Not hard enough to knock me down, but all my books and papers get dumped on the ground. And stepped on and kicked and shoe-smashed into the ground. Kathy Diggers, her charcoal-and-green-rimmed eyes practically dancing, is jumping up and down in her new PUMAs on my zippered loose-leaf book like she is on a trampoline. My luck, just today my mother stuffed a tuna sandwich into my book.

The only good thing is watching Myrna, fighting to get her licks in, get "accidentally" kicked by Maryanne. All the while I'm trying to hang on to my backpack by locking my arms tight against my chest, but it gets picked off me, and

Maryanne, who looks like she's training for the Olympics, flings it halfway across the lawn.

I'm not even fighting back, I'm just trying to hang on to my things. But it doesn't work, and when they get it all, they just back off, and walking like nothing happened, follow their leader up the steps into the school.

I'm standing here, like, stunned. I can't believe this is really happening. I mean, this is high school. We're almost adults. And I know people were passing by. But nobody helped me. How come?

And another weird thing, Jeanette Sue never even touched me. Is she scarier than ever or what?

I pick up my papers and books, which are a mess, all torn and dirty, especially the loose-leaf with the squashed sandwich seeping out of the zipper. I don't even want to look at my English report inside.

I am reaching for the last book when a hand beats me to it. I know even before I look up that it's his hand. In the instant before I have to look at him, I scramble to figure out what I should do. I know what I'd like to do, but sinking my teeth into his hand is not in the plan.

I look up and squeeze my face into a smile. He leaps back. A flash of horror pops his brown eyes wide open. I pull my fangs back and undo the smile and say, "Hey, thanks," without choking.

"What happened? What did you do, fall or something?" I can't resist, so just like in a movie, I look into his eyes—my face, like, a nose away from his—and say, "I guess I did fall." And keep staring at him.

And he stares back at me and it's like we're both locked there. Like some invisible hands are holding my face right there. And it's hot. My face, I mean, not just hot sexy, you know, but temperature hot.

I'm absolutely still, but I feel him closing the space between us. And then some car horn blows in the distance and he turns his face and his lips just barely brush mine. Or maybe they didn't. Maybe I just felt the heat go past me.

Then it's over. We both stand up. Uncomfortable.

He wants to help me, but I don't let him. I grab the book from his hand and race up the steps and into the building. I don't look back. But I can feel him looking at me.

Even after the door closes behind me, I feel his presence. It takes me halfway to my class to remember this is all about getting Jeanette Sue.

By the time I get to the second floor, the bell has rung, and even though I practically fly down the halls, I'm late for English.

Normally, English is totally my best subject. At least it was in Lubbock, but here I've got Jeanette Sue and four of her ticks sucking the blood out of it, so now it's my worst.

"Twyla Gay, do you have your Edgar Allan Poe report?" That's Ms. Helburt, the teacher.

You mean Tuna Fish Poe? It was so greasy I had to throw it out. I don't tell her that. All I say is, "I forgot." I'm not going to start tattling like a baby.

She's not pleased, she wants to know why. But I just shrug my shoulders and mumble something, I don't even know what.

Ms. Helburt is okay, but very teacher. She even wears teacher clothes, browns and tans, and teacher shoes in browns and tans with sensible heels. She's so teacher that you figure when school lets out, she just evaporates into thin air. She's absolutely not a person you could talk to, not that I could tell her what happened, so I just have to listen to a lecture on late papers and how that's a thousand demerits that will follow me through my life and probably end up on my gravestone.

I don't know why she doesn't seem to hear the giggles and twitters from those butthead RCs.

Steve Dennis, Ryder's friend, is in the seat next to me. He tries to commiserate, but I pay no attention. Out of the corner of my eye I can see him sniffing around trying to find out where the fish smell is coming from. The only nice thing about him is that he thinks the smell is coming from him, which is kind of sweet. Still, I don't help him.

The interminable class finally ends, and I shoot out straight to the bathroom to try and wash some of the tuna grease out of my loose-leaf. At least it oiled the zipper.

Myrna Fry

Jeanette Sue called an emergency meeting of the RCs this morning before school. Right away, before anyone else can, I go, "Hey, that dance you did on Saturday night was fabulous and the flying stuff at the end was, like, totally great. You gotta teach me."

And right away she stopped everything and showed me, and wow, I went flying practically across the room. It wasn't as good as what she did on the bar, but if I practice, I could do it better. And if the wall wasn't so close, I wouldn't slam into it so hard.

As soon as I got up, I went, "Thanks a mil."
Is she the best?

Anyway, the plan was for trashing Twyla Gay's books and stuff, and it went great. I mean, we were like a team. There's no way she's going to be able to use any of that stuff today.

Like in English now. Ms. Helburt was really pissed because she didn't have the Edgar Allan whoever paper. I got mine off the Net. You know, the Ask Jeeves thing. Like she's ever going to look it up.

I tried to read it, but poetry sucks, and you know, like, hello, so what if ravens talk. I already knew that.

Besides, who cares? More important things are happening. I overheard Jeanette Sue talking to Maryanne. Actually, J. S. would have told me herself, but Maryanne is so jealous of me that she dies every time I get included in stuff, so J. S. just makes sure she says it where I can overhear them.

I mean, she had to know I was in the toilet when they were at the mirror talking. Okay, I was there before they came in, but I just know J. S. could tell I was there, because we're really very close, like there's, like, this telepathy thing between us. And what she said only proves that she was pretending she didn't know I was there, you know, making up phony things like saying how I'm dumpy and have horrendous taste in clothes and that my mother is skinny, ugly, and plays around, and my stepfather is a dickhead. She had to throw in some real things too, like about my stepfather. I think she so fooled Maryanne, like totally.

Anyway, J. S. goes how we, the RCs, are going to get Twyla Gay and Deena and finish them off. Like major enough to make them want to transfer, and it's all happening Wednesday in the lunchroom.

Except she didn't say how.

Two days. I can hardly wait.

CHAPTER 23

Twyla Gay

It's lunchtime, and Deena and I have been waiting up in the stadium for almost an hour and nobody is showing up. And I don't think they're going to. Every time anyone comes out of the building and sees us, they shoot right back in. We're poison.

I'm seething, I'm so out-of-my-mind furious. Every time I think of that horrendous stuff with my books this morning, I could totally scream.

Something nasty is definitely going on; all kinds of secret whispering with the RCs. And a lot of buttheads looking at me and Deena and pointing and giggling and rolling their eyes.

I told Deena what happened with J. S. this morning, and she says the RCs are, like, on a rampage. They attacked her in history first period before the teacher got there, and started with the slut stuff.

"You know, with lots of really horrendous details, like *Sex and the City* is nothing compared to those creeps. And then they're going on about how I had these breast implants and was that before or after my abortions, and more about how I gave this guy an STD."

I can see she's totally on the brink of breaking down.

"And you know what?" she says. "Maybe I don't want this anymore."

"What do you mean?"

"I mean I could go to a boarding school. My parents would send me. They offered."

"Do you want to?"

"Of course I don't. I want to stay home."

"Let me get this right. Jeanette Sue is going to make you go away to boarding school even though you don't want to."

"Maybe she is."

"Boy, that pisses me off. Her running our lives. Well, not my life. I'm so not going to let her."

It's not like Deena's a coward. It's hard enough being Hispanic in a practically all-white school. On top of that she's had her life destroyed for the last two years. And nobody even helped her. I like how tough I sound, but it's sort of a little like cheating, because I don't really have a choice. I'm stuck here.

"Okay," I admit, "maybe I have to stay, but I don't have to fight. That's my choice. And I'm not going to fight fair, either, I'm going to fight just the way they do, only way better."

I guess that sounded pretty impressive. I hope I'm not fooling her and myself.

"You really going to fight them?"

"Yeah, I'm going to kick ass."

"No matter what?"

"Jeanette Sue or bust."

"Okay," she says, and now she's smiling, and it's a nice mean smile. "Then, me too."

"The first thing we've gotta do is take that slut stuff and ram it down their throats."

"How?"

"I don't know. . . ."

"Great start."

". . . yet. Hey, look how fabulous we were last night. We didn't go there with a plan. It just came to us."

"Well, maybe one of our many minions will come up with something brilliant." And she spreads her arms to include all the empty benches. "Right, guys?"

"Well, we're not going to enlist any troops up here. We've got to get down with the masses."

"I hate the masses."

"It's okay, they hate you, too. And me."

It's like we both had a big shot of adrenaline, the way we take those steps going down. We're a great team.

Except I still haven't told her about my plan with Ryder. I don't know why.

The two of us, we are, like, totally determined, so we go straight to the hall outside the lunchroom to catch the kids coming out. No one even stops to listen to us. Finally Tammy Johnson comes out. She's sort of our last hope. Actually a pretty good hope. But before we can get to her, Kathy Diggers and two other RCs, Maryanne and Betty Jane, cut us off.

"Hey," Kathy says to Tammy, real friendly like, "cool glasses."

"Thanks," Tammy says, barely stopping.

"No," Kathy says, "thank you."

And just like that, she whips them off Tammy's face. Tammy is stunned. Us too. She stands there with her mouth open for a second and then makes a grab for them.

"Hey," she says, "what are you doing? They're mine."

And then Kathy, like, starts to examine them and shakes her head. "I don't think so. Unless your name is Coach. Is it Coach?"

And her two moron friends break up.

"Give them to me!" Tammy shouts, and tries to take them back, but Kathy, who is at least five ten, holds them up high in the air while Betty Jane and Maryanne grab Tammy's arms and shove her back against the wall.

We're sort of standing there like dummies. Then Deena says to me, "So?"

And I say, "Yeah!" And we both make a dive for the glasses. Betty Jane and Maryanne let go of Tammy and it's a free-for-all. We're all jumping for the glasses.

Kathy starts to take off, but Deena sticks her foot out and Kathy stumbles close enough so I grab one end of the glasses and give it a real pull. And she pulls her end.

And of course, just like a wishbone, the glasses snap.

"You are going to so regret this! All of you!" Kathy shouts and flings her half of the $60 glasses right at my head. I catch it before it hits me.

"Gee, Tammy, I'm really sorry. I was only trying to help you. . . ."

"Hey, I'd rather have broken glasses than let that bitch have them. Thanks for helping me anyway. I think maybe it's a first."

We all smile at one another. Feeling pretty good.

"Enjoy it while it lasts," Tammy says. "You know they're going to kill us."

"Are you afraid?" I ask her.

"Yeah, aren't you?"

"Not so much now that there are three of us."

"Hey, wait. I'm so not part of this. All I want to do is get in and get out. I'm thinking college, that's all."

"College. Right . . ." Think! Fast! "I shouldn't tell you. . . ."

What shouldn't I tell?

"What shouldn't you tell?"

This is no fooling-around fighting for my life. You have to be ready to think fast and lie. "About the study . . . all you have to know is that it's going to help all of us."

Deena looks at me real weird, but she doesn't say anything. She's waiting for Tammy to ask.

And she does. "What study?"

"I can trust you. You know that thing about high school bullies. Mean girls."

"I don't know what you're talking about, do you?" Tammy looks at Deena, who finds something weird on her sneaker and starts scraping her foot on the floor.

We both watch for a couple of seconds, and then I say, "I guess I'm not supposed to say anything."

"About what?" Tammy's getting a little irritated.

"Swear you won't tell anyone?"

"Go on. I swear."

Deena's no help. She's still busy scraping imaginary poop off her shoe.

"There's this study about bullies—"

"Yeah, you said that. So?"

"That guy down there . . . ," I say, nodding in the direction of a tall, skinny, older man mopping the floor. Even Deena stops scraping long enough to look.

"The janitor?"

"Not. I could get in such trouble for this."

"So if he's not a janitor, what is he?"

"An undercover inspector from the Board of Ed."

Deena just stares at me like it's the first time she ever saw me and would like it to be the last. I'm in the fight mode and nothing is going to stop me.

I talk really fast. "They're picking fifteen girls to become part of, like, an undercover group to out the bullies. As a reward these girls will be given a special recommendation in the form of an aclaimane."

Do you love it? Aclaimane. It just came to me and it's perfect. Definitely sounds totally academic. Not that I've never lied before, but this is so, I don't know, calculated. Now there's no stopping me.

"That's a special thing recognized only by college admissions people, to be attached to your college applications and signed by the president of the Board of Ed. Additionally, a full four-point course with an A will be included, along with a fully paid-for trip to Los Angeles and the set of *Gilmore Girls* and then a day out with . . ."

Out of the tiniest slice of peripheral vision I can see Deena shaking her head, and even though I can't see her rolling her eyes, I can sense she is, so I pull back a little. It really doesn't matter, since when they find out, the Hollywood lie will be the least of it.

"Sorry, that's been cancelled."

"The *Gilmore Girls?*" Tammy is with me one hundred percent.

"No, not that, just the additional day."

"Hey," she says, "it all sounds awesome and I absolutely want to be part of it."

"Deena?" Would you believe she's back to the poop on her shoe? "Can we get Tammy in? Deena?"

I tap her on her shoulder and she looks up with a wild look in her eyes.

"Hel-lo. Can we get Tammy in?" I repeat.

Deena studies Tammy for a minute. It looks like she's going to blow it. But then she doesn't.

"Absolutely," she says.

She's with me.

"Remember," I tell her, "not a word. Especially to him." I'm pointing to the janitor, who is definitely not impressive. And a lousy sweeper, too, papers and stuff all over the floor, which is good for me. Shows he's so not a real janitor.

"We're all meeting at five this afternoon . . ." I look at Deena.

". . . at my house." She jumps right in.

And just like that, we're in action. Tammy takes off, making a wide circle around the janitor.

Only twelve more people to go.

Deena and I go off in different directions. We have a lot of work to do before this afternoon. Like spreading the secret about the study. Spreading a rumor—especially one that's not true—is, like, really easy. And it goes around even faster if you swear them to secrecy.

I'm running all over the place trying to grab people when they get out of class. So far Sally Lynn Walker and Ashley Bauer have said yes. Janni wanted to know if April Elliott and Jessica Kramer were going, and when I said yes, she said okay. Then I hit Jessica and April and told them Janni was going, and they said okay too.

This lying thing is awesome. It's got great possibilities. Especially useful in destroying enemies.

I've got my five, not counting Tammy, plus Deena's two that makes ten. All we need is five more. I should have said the study needed twenty. Costs the same.

"Hey, I've been looking for you."

Ryder. I spin around and end up with my face about six inches from the middle of his chest. He smells like soap. I love that.

"You ran off so fast this morning I didn't get to ask you . . ." I look up and he looks down. How could he have such soft, warm, really friendly, crinkly eyes and be such a shit?

"Yes?" I stay exactly where I am and he doesn't move either. It feels like we're, like, inside this warm bubble, alone.

" . . . if you want to go out tomorrow night?"

"Just the three of us—you, me, and Jeanette Sue?"

"Hey, look, yeah, we date but it's nothing. . . ."

"Okay."

"Okay, you'll go with me?"

"Yeah."

"Anything special you'd like to do?"

"I don't know. . . ."

"Well, I'll pick you up at seven and we can decide."

He'll probably dump me as soon as he sees my mansion, so I offer to meet him.

"That's all right, I've got the car. You're at the Vickery houses, right?"

Since that doesn't seem to turn him off, I give him my address and say, "See you tomorrow at seven." And take off.

Leave 'em wanting more!

Except I'm the one who wants more. Really lame, isn't it?

CHAPTER 24

Myrna Fry

It's like the whole school is whispering. And they totally stop as soon as they see me. Maybe they're planning a surprise party for me, except my birthday isn't until August. But they don't know that and I'm so not telling.

I gotta get my list of people I so don't want to come. The ones I wrote down in Mr. Webber's math class. You see, math comes in handy sometimes. I mean, those are badass people who would just ruin everything.

Like Twyla Gay, for starters. I heard she tried to take Kathy Diggers's sunglasses away, and then she, like, snapped them apart for no reason at all. How gross is that? Poor people really suck. They just don't want anyone to have what they can't have.

Jeanette Sue still hasn't told me my job for the humongous Wednesday slut thing in the lunchroom. But I know it's going to be big.

Boy, am I glad I'm so not a slut. There are a lot more sluts around than you think. You can always tell who they are because, like, the football stars and frat guys and all the most popular guys are calling them, like, all the time. I mean, it totally sucks having all those guys hanging around you at school and then waiting outside your classroom and, like, wanting to eat lunch with you and take you places in their cars. It's like they have to pretend it's so not just for the sex, so they, like, bring you presents and take you to the movies and parties and everything.

I mean, there's just no time when some great-looking guy—you know, like the Abercrombie & Fitch kind—isn't hanging around you. I would just hate that.

But if you were really a slut, you know what the best contraceptive is? Mountain Dew. You know, the drink. This girl told me she heard it works perfectly. She didn't say how much you have to drink, in fact, she didn't even say you had to drink it. I should ask because, like, maybe you don't drink it. Some guys were saying about Deena how one time she was having sex behind the tennis courts and it started to thunder and lightning, and just when it got really hot, the lightning hit them, and wow! The guy said it was fabulous. Except later I heard that they got stuck together, maybe from the lightning, and they had to call the fire department to unstick them.

Something's going on, and I don't mean just with the RCs. I heard some rumor about people joining a study. Duh. Like I would join a study. I am so not interested in any kind of study, but maybe I should try to get some info. I can because Twyla Gay still thinks I'm her best friend. In fact, I'm going to do it right now in social studies.

Twyla Gay

Here comes smiling Myrna, my favorite moron suck-up. Of course, she's not sucking up to me. She's on a mission and I can't wait to know what it is.

"Hey, Twyla Gay." You know how they used to describe people in books as perky? That's Myrna right now. Except phony perky is so weird looking. She's bobbing her head around like she's attached to a battery. Poor Myrna is always running to catch up to where she'll never catch up. "What's happenin'?" she wants to know.

I'm straining every muscle in my face not to look like I want to kill her.

"Nothing much," I tell her. "What's going on with Jeanette Sue?"

More smiles. She can't wait to tell me. I hope that canary she swallowed eats out her throat.

"The usual. You know, all kinds of parties and things like we have all the time. And then tomorrow night J. S. does her riding thing."

"Riding?" I know she has a horse, that's all that anybody ever talks about.

"The moonlight riding stuff she does on Tuesday nights. You know. At the club. Well, actually you wouldn't know. Anything special happening with you guys?" That's Myrna subtly digging.

"Nothing but your thing," I tell her. Of course, I have no idea what her thing is or even if she has a thing. I just figure from the secret look on her face that they're planning something horrendous.

"You mean the Wednesday thing?"

Bingo.

"You know already?" She's surprised.

"Of course. I guess Jeanette Sue is pretty sure I'm going to show up. Right?" I'm talking gobbledygook, but she answers me like it makes sense.

"Well, we figured everyone has to go to the lunchroom anyway," she says, pretending like she's part of the plan, which I would swear she isn't. "Deena's coming too, right?"

She's like a dream prisoner of war. Ask one question and she spills everything. I play dumb, which I am because I have no idea what she's talking about.

"I don't know." Which is the first honest thing I've said.

"You kidding? She's what it's all about."

"What do you mean?"

"Hey, you know, even sluts eat lunch."

And like she's just pulled off some big coup, she throws her head back á la Jeanette Sue, turns, nearly slamming into the wall, and takes off.

Myrna Fry

Wow, like, that was so way easy. I mean fooling Twyla Gay. Funny, but I never noticed that she has the nastiest eyes. They feel like they could burn right through you. Even though she was smiling, she looked like she wanted to kill me. Anyone else but Twyla Gay and I'd be scared. But she's just sucking up to us RCs.

Twyla Gay

Getting information from Myrna is like a snap. She tries so hard to make me think she's an insider, but I know the truth. And so I just watched her standing there with the little sweat beads hanging on her almost mustache, all excited to be such a big shot and ending up such a dummy. If I were the nice person I used to be before these skanks made my life so miserable, I would have felt sorry for her. Except that part of me is gone.

I probably could have gotten the whole plan out of her, but she gave me all I really need: The lunchroom Wednesday and it has something to do with Deena. It fits our plans perfectly.

And the best part is the stuff about Jeanette Sue going riding. Moonlight riding.

I call Ryder and tell him I decided what I want to do tomorrow night.

"Horseback riding," I tell him.

"At night?"

"Yeah, moonlight horseback riding. I love it. Do it all the time."

"No kidding."

"Why? You think just because I don't live in HighlandPark that I couldn't horseback ride?"

"I didn't mean that . . . I . . ."

"I happen to be a champion. You belong to that club, don't you?"

"My parents do. Hey, okay, then it's moonlight riding tomorrow. I'll pick you up at seven."

It's a twofer, knocking off Jeanette Sue and Ryder both at once.

Later that afternoon I get a lift with my aunt Willa to Deena's house. The house isn't as fabulous as Jeanette Sue's, but it's still awesome and I like it even better. None of the houses around here are really old, but if you didn't know any better, you'd think hers was. It's like something from a movie about the old South, white clapboards with two fat, round pillars that hold up a portico over the entrance. It's got shutters, too, in a taupy color with a beige trim, and a circular driveway, and I love circular driveways. They're so elegant. It probably doesn't look that elegant when my aunt's eleven-year-old Taurus pulls around, but from inside the car, it feels just as good.

Deena is waiting for me, and as soon as I open the car door, she comes out. It's a very different Deena outside of school. She's really friendly to my aunt, and it's like she's my best friend, the way she takes my hand and walks me into the house.

She's got a little brother, Luis, a cute kid with these really deep dimples when he smiles. He's about the same age as my cousin William. I don't know why I thought she was an only child. Probably because she seemed so alone at school. It's really vile what those shitheads did to her. I so want to get them.

I meet her mom and dad, and they're real friendly and nice, but definitely regular parent types. Like very involved. We're not there three minutes and Mr. Lopez is already giving us a list of helpful instructions for our meeting. Deena says he can't help himself, he's a lawyer. Like all the time. Her mom is really pretty with very short curly hair. Luis has her dimples, and Deena has her sparkly dark eyes. She also has her boobs, except Mrs. Lopez wears tight T-shirts that really show them off and Deena tries to lose hers in big shirts.

"Your parents must really hate Jeanette Sue and all those assholes for what they did to you," I say when we get to her room.

"They don't know anything about it."

My jaw drops. "All this time and you didn't tell them?"

"You told your mom?"

"No, but . . ."

"Same reasons, I'm sure. It's disgusting to have to tell your parents things like that, and then they'd shoot up to school and start making a huge scene. And it would ruin everything for me at home. I would be the poor picked-on weirdo, and maybe they might think it was true, I mean the slut thing."

"I guess," I say. I guess it's sort of the same reasons I didn't tell anyone in my house. You feel so embarrassed and then everybody's thinking, like, poor you. It's like it makes it official that you're an undesirable.

I purposely got here early so we could discuss our plans, just Deena and me. The idea is mine, but Deena is financing it. We have to throw her little brother out at least six times. He's kid-brother nosy, asking a million questions. We have no time to fool around, we have only one day, tomorrow, Tuesday, to get everything set up and ready for Wednesday at lunch.

We decide to tell the other guys only half of the plan so that they don't accidentally let it out. Tell fifteen people a secret and it's so not a secret. This thing is not going to work unless it's an absolute knock-'em-out surprise.

Tammy is the first one here. And then two minutes later Sally Lynn Walker and Ashley Bauer come in with April Elliott. And then Janni and Jessica Kramer and the rest of them dribble in. I can hardly believe it, but they all show up. I was scared nobody would show.

And the weird thing is, it's really a nice group. Okay, they're not all beauties like the RCs. Like that matters anyway. The important thing is that they're not cookie-cutter people, they look like regular girls. Jessica Kramer is petite and April Elliott must be almost five ten and Janni is a few pounds over-weight and Ashley still has braces and Sally Lynn is Asian and way the best-looking, but so what? You forget all of that in five minutes. The best thing about them is that they're really smart, a lot smarter than those moron followers of Jeanette Sue. But it's like they're so intimidated that they don't really use their brains.

Funny, but with all these totally great girls around, all I ever saw was Jeanette Sue and her gang. It's like the Ruling Class dominates the whole school and turns it into a horren-dous prison with them as monster matrons.

Deena's dad brings back pizzas and soda and some Krispy Kremes, and we laugh and dish and watch *Scary Movie* and dish about Avril Lavigne, and Ashton Kutcher and Demi. How weird is that? And how fishnet tube tops are out and we're all going to throw out our white Louis Vuitton bags when we get home. Lucky me, I tell them, I never owned one anyway. And they all break up. Me too. Best of all is that we have an awesome time. It's like nobody really knew Deena, which is weird because she's been in the school two years. It's so fun we almost forget why we're here.

Like I said, we aren't planning to tell them everything, just enough to keep them interested. Deena starts off saying about the big whatever the RCs are planning for Wednesday in the lunchroom. They want to know what it is, but we don't know, so we tell them it doesn't matter because we have a secret weapon.

"Like what?" Tammy wants to know.

"You'll get the stuff on Wednesday morning."

"Like what stuff?"

"That's all we can say now," I tell her.

That's when they go ballistic. April Elliott shakes her head. "No way. You expect us to just go into this blind? I mean, this is Jeanette Sue. She'll, like, eat us alive."

Now all these great girls, our new wonderful friends, totally turn on us. All shaking their heads at the same time. No way.

"Okay, here's the deal. Wednesday morning we give you the stuff and tell you what's happening. Nobody says you have to do it. Maybe you like things the way they are now."

There's a big silence.

"I hope this isn't about the study, because that's bullshit," Tammy says.

"We only did it to get your interest," I tell her. "I'm really sorry, but we needed your help."

Then Deena asks straight out, "Will you help us?"

Nobody says no but nobody really commits, and it sort of, like, ruins the evening, so there's nothing left to do but go home.

I wait till everybody leaves to talk to Deena. I tell her we have no choice, we have to go ahead with our plan, otherwise Jeanette Sue will make our lives even worse than they are now.

"I'm ready," she says, "even if it's just the two of us. But I have to tell you, if this doesn't work, I'm leaving. I'm really sorry."

I tell her, "Okay, I understand."

Like we arranged, we tell her parents that we're doing the costumes for a show, and Mrs. Lopez is so happy that Deena is finally getting involved in school activities that she can't do enough. She has a friend who owns a textile company, and she calls her and arranges to get the T-shirts we need, and they can even print what we want on them too, though they're a little surprised at our choice. Her parents are totally cool about helping, but still they're, like, very confused about what kind of a show this is, especially when we tell them we need the shirts to look like they have breasts inside. The way we explain it, they think it's just weird high school humor. But mostly they're like parents and their big interest is in talking about why we waited so long to do the work. And then there's a little bit in Spanish between Deena and her dad and then back to English, so I can hear how we should have started last week and why do we leave things for the last minute. This is a problem for Deena. Nice to know she's just normal like everyone else.

After a lot of phone calls and stuff they figure out a way to get some foam rubber things that we can glue in the shirts, and everything can be ready Tuesday night, and we can assemble them Wednesday morning really early, like seven o'clock, before school.

"You think everyone is going to go with us?" I ask Deena.

"Absolutely. Once they see how fabulous our plan is, they're going to jump right in. It's a sure thing."

That's probably another flaw in my friend. Since she's recovered from her hopelessness, she's not just a half-full glass. She's over the top.

Twyla Gay

CHAPTER 26

Deena and I talk fifteen times on the phone Tuesday morning, and each time she talks me out of chickening out of my date with Ryder tonight. She thinks it's just a date. I never told her that he was the one driving the car that night at the mall. I'll tell her after. Maybe.

I hardly notice anything or anyone all day long. And I can't concentrate in any of my classes. It's weird, but I don't even run into Ryder. But that doesn't stop me from thinking about him. I wish it weren't the way it is. I wish I didn't have to pay him back. Wouldn't it be nice just to go on a date with him? I wish he weren't such crud, but he is. Is there something wrong with me that I'm attracted to such a lowlife?

William and my aunt are there when I get home in the afternoon. I haven't actually dealt with the bike thing yet. Everyone still thinks it was stolen from the yard. It was one of those lies by omission. Like I omitted to tell the truth. I will eventually tell them. Well, sort of, once I get the money. I'm trying to get a job in the sporting goods store in town, but I haven't heard yet. That's going to be the first thing I do with the money, a new bike for William. He's really a good kid, even though he does ask a lot of questions, but that's because he's very smart. It can be a pain sometimes, like tonight, when I'm trying to find my moonlight riding outfit.

"Is he your boyfriend?" he asks me, all the while jumping on my bed, his blond hair sailing up as he comes down. And then up again. He never seems to sit still.

"No way," I tell him. "Could you stop jumping on my bed?"

"So how come you're going on a date with him?"

He stops jumping up and down on the bed. Now he jumps from the bed to the closet door. Since my room isn't that big, I have to grab him before he slams into the door.

"It's too complicated."

"You always say that when you don't want me to know."

How come?"

"Cause I don't want you to know."

"How come?"

I try on a black scoop-neck blouse with beige lace all along the bottom and long sleeves that come down practically to the middle of my fingers that I've been saving for something really special, like the big dance at the club that I would never be invited to anyway, so why not wear it tonight? My mother would go bonkers if she knew I was wearing it for horseback riding. It was from a birthday present that she got from her boss and returned to get the money to buy me this blouse. I'm glad she's working tonight, so she doesn't see me in it.

"So, what do you think?"

"Cool."

"Do you think it's weird with the jeans?"

He takes a good long look. Suddenly, not like an eight-year-old, more like a guy, he's appraising me. Then he nods his approval. "Uh-uh."

I go with it.

I have no boots except ones with really chunky heels, and I'm certainly not wearing sneakers, so it's the heels. It's not like it's going to ruin my form or something. I don't know how to ride anyway. I've never been on a horse, except I have this picture of myself on a pony when I'm about, like, two, but I don't remember it at all. That's, like, my whole riding career. What's the big deal, anyway? These are trained horses. Anyone can ride them.

Ryder pulls up right in front of my house at exactly seven. It's like he knew where it was all the time. Funny thing, his car is a light blue and I thought it was red. That's what it looked like that night, but of course, it was very dark and the headlights were in my eyes. But it's a convertible. That much I saw. I don't want him to come in, not because I don't want him to see my house, it's just I don't want to introduce him to my aunt and William because I don't want anyone saying this creep is a nice guy. So I run right out as soon as I see him.

"Hey." He jumps out of the car like he's going to open the door for me, but I'm too fast.

"Hey," I say, opening the door and jumping in before he gets halfway around the front.

He gets back in the car and smiles at me, but there's something about the way he looks at me that's a little weird. Maybe the blouse was too much.

"What?" I say, like sort of challenging.

"Nothing. You look great."

Actually, he looks like he's happy to see me. Now his smile is, like, really big and it takes over his whole face.

"Yeah," he says, "totally."

Poor sucker has no clue. The way he acts, it's like he really thinks I forgot what he did. Never!

The club is totally elegant. I mean, right from the long road up through impeccable lawns and huge beds of magnificent-colored impatiens that trail alongside. There's a golf course on one side and a riding path on the other that goes off into a whole wooded area. We drive up to the front of the clubhouse and it looks like the White House. I mean, how pretentious is that? Valets in uniforms jump out to take the car and open the doors.

Ryder is friendly and knows their names, and they sort of fool around with him, you know, that arm-punching thing guys do. If you didn't know what a skank he was, you'd think he was a nice guy.

We walk through the lobby, which is very impressive, and on our way he introduces me to a couple of the members. And I'm smiling and friendly and really cool like I do this every day.

And then we go out the back entrance toward the stables. My heels keep sinking into the ground and making a weird sucking sound when I pull them out. The only thing to do is walk on my toes, which makes it really hard to keep my balance, so I end up leaning into Ryder every few steps. He thinks it's me being friendly.

"You ride English or Western?" he asks when we get to the stables.

I haven't got a clue, but I say English because when you've lived your entire life in Texas, anything Western is a total turnoff.

Ryder talks to the guy in charge, and some kid walks two horses out. I had no idea they would be so big. I was thinking more like the pony in my picture. Both horses look the same except for the saddles. I like the big one that looks more like an easy chair with places to hold on.

Turns out that's Western and mine, English, is this little tiny thing that you can slide right off.

Which I almost do the first time. Just like in a movie where the guy gets a lift onto the horse and goes right over. Except the kid helping me grabs on to my leg and holds me back. He thinks it's pretty funny, but I give him a killer look that wipes the smile off.

Luckily Ryder is busy fixing his saddle and doesn't see me. I have trouble right away with Cutie. A dumb name for such a huge animal. All he wants to do is eat. He's got his head so far down it's all I can do not to slide right over his neck and down his nose.

"The reins," the kid says, motioning his head toward I don't know what. "The reins."

I do like, *Huh?* And he picks up what is obviously the reins and puts them in my hands. I know what reins are, it's just I didn't see them hanging all the way down the horse's neck. Right away Cutie's not happy to stop eating and keeps shoving his neck out pulling on the reins, so the kid gives him a yank and he stops.

I hope he didn't think it was me.

"Let's go," Ryder says, pulling his horse around and taking off. Cutie, who is obviously a Myrna-type follower, follows, and we go flying. Well, not exactly flying, but even walking feels fast and dangerous up this high.

My sleeves are so long they get all bunched up in my fists with the reins, so it looks like I don't have any hands. And I'm bent over like a hook to have as much of me as possible close to the horse. The whole picture is totally unsexy, but Ryder doesn't seem to notice. He's busy talking about how wonderful sunset rides are. Like I could look up long enough to see it.

Someplace in the first thirty seconds Cutie decides he's had enough and turns to go back home. My heart is with him.

"Hey!" Ryder calls out. "Where you going?"

At the sound of his voice Cutie turns and goes over to him like a dog.

"What's happening?" he wants to know.

"Just trying to calm him down. I like them to get the feel of my hands."

He's impressed. Me too. Only Cutie isn't. He's too busy looking for the next meal.

We get to a crossroads. "Which way?" Ryder asks.

"Where do most people go?" I do not want to miss Jeanette Sue.

"Down toward the lake. It's got the best view."

And we go off toward the lake. Actually, I'm beginning to kind of like riding. I'm still hooked over, but now I'm able to move my head a little so that I can look around. Only the bottom part of everything, but I can see the best part, the lake and the reds and golds of the sun beginning to set.

Ryder starts to say how he used to go riding all the time, but he hasn't been for a long time and on and on, and I'm not really listening because I think I see her. Right up ahead. All by herself. Looking good, I have to say, sitting straight up on a beautiful horse that's sort of prancing and rearing his head. She looks like she's having a lovely time.

Until she sees us.

Then she stops dead, jerks her horse around until she's facing us. This is my big move time.

Like I really am a champion, I jerk on Cutie's reins and pull him around and head him in toward Ryder. Now I'm nose-to-nose with his horse. Well, not me, Cutie and whatever his horse is called, which is a surprise to Ryder but not as big as when I get alongside and lean over with my face up to his and my lips sticking out.

Okay, it's not a pretty sight, kind of like the handless hunchback moving in for a kiss, but he's so stunned he doesn't move away. In fact, he moves his face toward me. I lunge and miss and land a giant kiss on his shoulder instead, but it's good enough so that Jeanette Sue gets the picture.

I don't see the response, but I can hear it. There's a long, horrendous neigh that echoes around the lake and the sound of beating hooves. I'm assuming it's the horse.

Time to get out.

I pull hard on the reins to try to get my horse around so at least I can face the attack, but stupid Cutie nuzzles in closer to Ryder's horse and somehow my heel gets caught in one of the straps of Ryder's saddle. I try to pull it out, but I can't. This definitely sucks.

I peek up at Ryder and see him looking straight ahead, in horror, at the onslaught.

And then he looks down at me, still trapped against his horse with my shoe wedged in. And for a second he looks, like, totally quizzical, and then he gets it.

"You set this up."

"Right. This is for the car."

And just a nanosecond before Jeanette Sue hits, I pull old Cutie back and, just like it's second nature to me, jerk the reins up against his back and he takes off. We're racing down the path and it's awesome. I feel my hair whipping back and the wind shooting past me and I'm flying.

I can hear Ryder shouting, "What car?" and Jeanette Sue screaming, "Bitch! Stop!"

But no one can stop me. I'm riding like a champion, hunkering down like a jockey, looking fabulous, except for the missing boot, which I guess is still sticking out of Ryder's saddle straps.

I did it! I paid them both back!

And I'm not finished yet!

CHAPTER 27

Myrna Fry

This is it. Wednesday, the big day, and even bigger because Kathy Diggers just called me. This is the first time she ever called me at home. Or any other place. And just to talk, 'cause we're, like, close friends. So we're, like, talking and she's telling me about how Jeanette Sue and Ryder were at the club last night having a moonlight ride and being very romantic when, like, out of nowhere Twyla Gay comes rushing in, off-the-wall jealous, and she takes off her boot and tries to hit J. S., and Ryder grabbed it away and Twyla Gay ran off, and Jeanette Sue still has this really crappy boot from, like, Payless or Target. How gross is that? I mean, those shoes really suck and they're totally ugly. Why would anyone shop in those stores when you could just as easy go to Jimmy Choo or Coach?

I tried to ask Kathy about the RCs' big cafeteria thing today, but it was like we got disconnected. All I know is we gotta be there by twelve.

CHAPTER 28

Twyla Gay

Deena and I picked up the shirts at her mother's friend's house before seven this morning, and then we went back to Deena's and glued in the breasts. They looked awesome.

But when we got to school, nobody would take any of the packages. Not Ashley, nor Janni, nor Tammy; none of the girls who were at Deena's on Monday night. They made a lot of phony excuses, but we knew it was because they were just too scared.

We lost. Deena and I. We never even had a chance to try our plan. And worst of all, now I know the line has been crossed. It's going to get physical, like Monday morning when they attacked me on the lawn, only worse.

All I wanted to do here was to go to school, get good grades, and maybe get a scholarship to some college and get on with my life. It was my chance to change the way my whole family has been living. Nobody in my family ever went to college. I know that sounds weird today. You'd think from television and movies that everybody goes to college. But that's not true. There's a whole load of people, nonmoneyed, who can't. Forget about the tuition. They have to work to make money just to eat and pay the rent.

With my mother and my aunt working, I could have done it. I would have been the first one in my family to go, but they're driving me out, the RCs. It's like I don't have a choice. I don't want to have to worry that someone will jump me every time I go to the bathroom or if I'm late leaving school. And I'll be all alone. It's for sure no one will help me. They're too scared. And you know what? I'm scared too. It's so unfair. What did I ever do to them? Well, I guess it doesn't matter, there's nothing I can do about it now.

Deena will change schools because she can. But me, the only thing I can do is drop out.

When the bell rings for lunch, I tell Deena I'm not hungry and I'm not going to the cafeteria. And I'm sure not dragging these stupid packages of shirts.

"We have to," Deena says.

"Why? It's over."

"I know."

"So?"

"We have to go out spectacular. Something awesome they'll remember forever."

"I'm sorry, Deena, I know I got you into this, but—"

"Hey, I'm not sorry you did. I was sinking. Man, I was finished. Every day was misery. I began to think they were right. I *was* worthless. And then you saved me."

"But I didn't."

"Yeah, you did. You made me feel strong enough to laugh at them. And even at myself. Deena the S. I love it because I know it's not me. For two years I didn't do much laughing. And I missed it. And now I want one major last laugh. On them. Then we can run for our lives. Please, best friend, do it for us. For our dignity."

"Rubber breasts in T-shirts. That's dignity?"

"For us? Yes."

CHAPTER 29

Twyla Gay

I let her talk me into doing it. We drag the bags of shirts down to the lunchroom, but it's like they were waiting for us. As soon as we come in, the RCs, with Jeanette Sue in command, make like a moving wall that corrals us into this one table that's sort of isolated but facing the rest of the room. Like we're on stage alone. Obviously this is part of their grand scheme, and we fell right into it.

"Told you we shouldn't have gone," I whisper to Deena.

"We're not finished yet."

"You're nuts. We are so way finished."

"Excuse me." Jeanette Sue steps toward us and says in the sweetest princess voice you ever heard, sweeter than Snow White herself, "Deena?"

"Yeah." Deena makes it sound strong, but I know she's totally nervous.

What's that Jeanette Sue bitch got in mind? Whatever it is, it's got to be horrendous. And all we have to fight back with are some stupid shirts. And no one to wear them.

I can see our team, if you can call them that, inching back against the far wall in a terrified clot.

"We think," says the princess, "that you are giving Highland Park High a bad name. And that hurts us all."

And like on a silent command all the other RCs nod their heads in hurt agreement.

"Says who?" At least Deena is trying. I have to give her that.

"Everyone. You're a slut," she says, turning to the drooling gang of asshole guys standing alongside her. "Bobby Jim?"

"Gropes me every time I pass her in the hall. Hey, I like to do my own groping," says Bobby Jim Wilson—a skinny, totally ugly, zitty guy who nobody would ever want to grope—smiling and winking to his cohorts.

And all the moron cohorts laugh.

And then Tom Devons, an okay, ordinary-looking hanger-ona, gets into it. "I was getting my jacket and she grabs my hand and slides it into her blouse. By the way, those *cuchifritos* are real."

More moron laughter.

Deena is so still it's like she's frozen. I don't even see her breathing. And I'm the opposite; I'm on fire. I can feel the sweat bubbles on my upper lip and my forehead, but I don't move to wipe them. That would look too weak.

"Where did you bang her?" Ralph Warren asks Peter John Henry. And Peter John says, "Which time?"

And Walter Whitman says to Deena, "Remember that alcove near the janitor's office? Totally great. Man, I came twice."

Now it's all happening so fast, every guy is practically shouting out these disgusting things, like one on top of another. And the girls are in it now, calling out, "Slut! Slut!" And we're just standing there.

Finally I explode. "Liars!" I shout at them.

But it's too late. They're like a lynching mob.

"Should I tell you about the scar she has on her ass?" Walter Whitman spits it right in my face.

"It's not true! It's a lie!" I keep shouting over and over again.

"It's a goddamned lie!" It's a guy's voice. And for an instant that sort of stops everyone.

"You're a goddamned liar, Whitman." It's Ryder. And he pushes through the crowd and, towering over Walter Whitman, who actually seems to shrivel a little, says right in his face, "You're a virgin and you know it." He doesn't touch him, but you can feel the force of his threat. "Right, Whitman? You're a virgin."

Whitman looks around for help, but his cohorts have noticeably taken a step back. He's on his own.

"Well . . . maybe."

"So you're lying about Deena, right?"

"Well, everybody else . . ."

Just like a prosecuting attorney, Ryder lights into him, "Yeah, but you didn't, right?"

"Not personally . . ."

"Yes or no. Did you have sex with Deena? Or anybody else in your life?"

It gets very silent, if silent can be very.

"No," he finally says, so low only the people close by can hear.

"I didn't hear that," Ryder says.

"No." This time Walter says it louder.

And now Ryder turns on Peter John, who instantly turns chicken. "Not me personally," he says, "but that's what I heard. Right, guys?"

But the guys are busy protecting themselves shrugging their shoulders like, *I don't know. . . .*

"Well, she's still a slut." Jeanette Sue steps forward, not at all afraid of Ryder.

"Then, so am I!" a voice from behind us shouts, and we all turn around and there is Tammy Johnson with the SLUT shirt on. Boobs sticking out like a platform, proudly presenting the word SLUT printed in red all across the top.

And now all the other girls, our team, are grabbing shirts and diving into them. I didn't even see them come out of their corner. Then someone throws me two shirts, and I give one to Deena and pull on the other. Now everyone, not just our team, but the bystanders, is grabbing the shirts, practically fighting over them. All shouting, "Me too!"

But the best is Ryder and Steve, who have somehow managed to squeeze themselves into the shirts, breasts and all. And they're loving it.

If only I could forgive him for the mall business. But I can't. I don't care that he came through when we needed him. It's unforgivable what he did to me.

The lunchroom is, like, total bedlam, with shirts flying around and everyone jumping up and down and shouting, "Me too!" or "Hey, look at me! I'm a slut!" It's like there's no stopping us.

I see Anna Marie sitting with Dawn and Joanne, the RC outcasts, terrified of Jeanette Sue and now just as afraid of us. I love watching them suffer.

"Throw 'em a shirt." Deena pokes me and motions to the three losers.

"No way. Let 'em rot," I tell her.

"Are we going to be the RCs now?"

"We'll be the good RCs."

"Good bullies? That's an oxymoron."

"A combination of opposites. I was in that English class too. But this time it's wrong. The way we'd run the school, nobody would have to be afraid of anyone. We'd make sure things ran the right way."

"Our way?"

"I don't think that makes us bullies. It just puts some fist into the good side."

Why does the good side always have to be such pushovers, so gentle and understanding? That's why the Jeanette Sues can eat us for breakfast. I think we have to be faster and stronger. Don't get me wrong, the strength I'm talking about isn't physical contact, it's using the power of courage.

"Okay"—I give this one to Deena—"I'll go with you on this." And I throw some shirts to Anna Marie, who looks like she's going to cry, but she doesn't. She smiles. All three do.

But I don't do it out of forgiveness. I do it to get three more people on our side. It's okay that Deena and I don't agree completely. Maybe it makes a good combination: gentle and understanding, and strong and vigilant. Either that or it's a super oxymoron.

I look around and it's totally incredible. There must be, I don't know, twenty of us. All in SLUT shirts and looking totally beautiful. The tide has turned. I know it because my barometer, Myrna Fry, has changed sides. Unfortunately, in true Myrna style, she did it so fast she's got the shirt on backward, with the breasts sticking out of her back like a camel. That kind of dumb can't be defeated, it can only be used.

Now we start moving. We're like an army making a frontal attack, pushing slowly but powerfully right into the center of the RCs. We don't even get to them when they break and run.

Jeanette Sue is the last. She has guts, but even she can't meet this power. Just when I'm about a nose from her, she bolts and runs out of the cafeteria after her defeated RCs.

We wiped them out. They will never rule again.

Everybody's jumping up and down, shouting, and dancing the football winner's dance. I see the teachers trying to quiet everyone, but there's no way. Besides, I think they're not sorry to see the RCs go either.

I get so carried away I leap up on the table. "We took back the school! It's ours!"

"Let's keep it!" Deena shouts.

It's awesome. Everybody going ballistic, clapping and cheering like it's some kind of fabulous championship. And maybe it is.

I start to get down from the table, when somebody puts his hands on my waist and lifts me down. It's Ryder, of course.

"Don't touch me," I tell him, and he backs off, shocked.

"And don't look so surprised. You think because you do one good thing that I'll forget the mall?"

"What are you talking about? What mall?"

"When Jeanette Sue tricked me into waiting at the mall. You were driving."

"No way. I don't even know what you're talking about. That wasn't me."

"Liar."

"Ask Steve."

174

"What? So he can lie for you?"

Steve comes over and Ryder asks him what he knows about some business at the mall. He says he doesn't know, and then he says, "Wait a minute. Was that the big trick Jeanette Sue played on someone?"

"On me," I say.

"That was Wilson who drove them. A red convertible, right? He hasn't shut up about it yet."

I did think it was a red car. And Bobby Jim is just the kind of gross-out to do something like that. But Steve is Ryder's best friend.

"Hey, Wilson!" Ryder calls out over the crowd. Way in the back I see Bobby Jim duck down. Ryder sees too and dives in, makes his way through, and comes right back with Bobby Jim.

"Tell her," he says, dragging him by the arm.

"What should I tell her?"

"The mall."

"Hey, it was just a joke. No big deal."

"Get out of here, you asshole," Ryder says, giving him a head-start shove that sends him falling into the crowd, who stand him up and, like a choreographed dance, spin him along until he hits free space. We can see him reeling and then stopping himself, taking one look back at the angry mob and fleeing.

"So?" Deena the S. says to me, sticking out her chest. "Now what do you think?"

"I think that shirt may not be for you. On the other hand, for me . . ."

But Ryder answers instead, "Not bad."

"Not the shirts, dummies, us," Deena says. "What do you think? We did it, didn't we?"

"Yeah," I say, and hug her with all my might but with the added padding, I can't get closer than two feet. And she can barely reach her arms around me.

But it's good enough. In fact, it's great. Nothing has ever been so great.

Myrna Fry

You remember how right from the start I liked Twyla Gay, but I couldn't bear to hurt Jeanette Sue's feelings? She needed me. And I'm just that kind of person who can't stand to see anyone hurt. I'm always standing up for the little guy. I'd probably be good in one of those mentor programs they're always pushing at school. Hey, I'd sign up in a heartbeat if they could get rid of all those needy little children with those terrible clothes. It's really heartbreaking. They have no taste at all.

"Hey! Twyla Gay! Deena! Wait up for me!"